# OMINOUS WHISPERS

## TAMMY GACH

# DEDICATION

To Michael Gach, for your patience, love, and support.
Your unwavering belief in me has made this book
possible.

# ACKNOWLEDGMENTS

Thank you to:

Matt Schwarck for your tireless editing, and for being the little brother that I never had, Kris Kline for your editing, and for making me a better writer, Samii Gach for your amazing artwork, Marcia Erhardt for your much needed input, and Douglas W. Daech, a brilliant author whose help was invaluable.

# OMINOUS WHISPERS

**It would be foolish to deny that a symbiotic relationship exists between people and their dwellings. When the human organism exudes positive energy, the host dwelling absorbs that energy, and it is beneficial for both the organism and the host. However, when the human organism exudes negative energy, the human becomes nothing more than a parasite who will, over time, destroy the dwelling, and the host will die.**

# PROLOGUE

Have you ever noticed that everything seems to shift into slow motion at the moment of a physical or emotional impact? You know the feeling. Your senses open up and become flooded with details of your surroundings. Things that take only fractions of a second in reality, play out like a slow motion movie, frame by frame in the traumatized mind. This time warp of perception was about to happen to seventeen year old Ted Greer.

When Ted walked into the Warren Bank on that hot and humid 24$^{th}$ day of August in 1978, he had no reason to notice that there were exactly four customers and three

1

tellers going about their business. He was as relaxed and comfortable as the tattered, lace-less canvas sneakers that covered his bare feet. Nothing drew his attention to the white marble floor with gray streaks through it, or made him notice that it was so highly-polished that you could see yourself in it. He walked along the pathway leading from the front door to the teller counter, but had not yet tuned into the fact that the path was lined with red carpet walkway mats that were so new that you could still smell the rubber backing. It was just a normal day with normal occurrences passing by him mostly unnoticed for now. The only thing he noticed, or cared to notice for that matter, was his girlfriend of the past two years, Sandy Crane, who was one of the three tellers on duty that afternoon.

Ted watched Sandy as she interacted with her customers at the counter. As always, her conversation was effortless and her genuine warmth left strangers feeling as if they had known her their entire lives. *God she's beautiful.* He thought, as he studied the way her full lips moved as she spoke, and the way the waves in her long chestnut brown hair danced upon her shoulders as she moved. He could smell the fragrance of her shampoo in his mind as he imagined nuzzling and kissing her neck. When he saw that she had noticed him standing in line, and was waving to him, he cleared his throat, and snapped out of his lust-filled daydream. Ted smiled and winked at her in his slow, relaxed style. He reminded her of an antebellum southern gentleman – like she had seen in movies – soft spoken, polite, and easy in his mannerisms – the kind of guy who made the southern belles swoon.

Sandy did not need to use words with Ted. When he looked at her, the smile and the love that shined back at him from her eyes spoke to him more honestly than any words ever could.

As Ted started to step forward in line, he noticed Sandy look past him toward the front door. The sparkle in her eyes was extinguished, and her pupils widened so quickly that her eyes appeared suddenly black and terrified. It was the first frame of what now seemed like a slow motion movie being thrust upon his senses, frame by horrible frame. The impact came before anyone even had a chance to scream, and it made his skin feel like it felt the time he had a cooler of ice water dumped on him at a picnic. He cringed and felt small, still watching Sandy's huge black eyes which now panned the room left to right and back again for what seemed like a minute, but was really less than two seconds. Then, the next frame of the horror movie was thrust upon him hard, as the sickening void of shocked silence was shattered.

# TAMMY GACH

"Get down! Everyone but the tellers! Down on the floor! Don't make me shoot you!" a man behind him shouted. The terrified cries and prayers of the seven other people in the bank played like macabre background music as they did what he demanded. Ted could see and hear each person individually, even though their cries were a cacophony of combined terror. The man stepped around the people on the floor and went up to the counter. He threw an army green duffel bag at the teller to Sandy's right.

"You three, put all the money in the bag one at a time! And if you put any of those dye packs in there, or hit any alarms, everybody dies!"

He was still shouting even though he did not need to. He was a huge man, at least six foot five and three hundred pounds, and he had a shotgun with the barrel sawed off short. In this split second of terror, everything about the man hit Ted's senses with nauseating detail. He was wearing a black knit ski mask, a camouflage green jacket, light brown corduroy bell bottom pants, work gloves that looked like deer skin, and well-worn brown Frey Brand boots-exactly like the ones Ted had at home. As it slowly seemed to play out, frame by hideous frame, all of the things to which Ted had paid no attention mere minutes ago, were now sensed in their entirety. He could smell the rubber of the new carpet mats. His eyes absorbed the color

4

of the marble, and a chill crept over his skin when he felt how cold the air conditioning had made the floor feel. The grotesque smell of cheap cologne from the man lying near him, assaulted his nose as it combined with the pungent body odor of the gunman, who must have been sweating like a pig in the ninety degree heat, beneath the heavy clothing that masked his identity.

Once the tellers were done putting the money in the bag, the man barked again. "Now you three, out here and down on the floor with the others!" They did as he said, and Sandy tried to get as close to Ted as she could. From a back office, behind where the tellers had just been standing, Alfred Willis, the bank's president appeared. A tall obese man, used to being the one in charge and barking the orders, Willis bellowed even louder than the gunman. "What the hell's going on?" Willis stood there for a moment, staring at the gunman. His brows furled, and his face a deep red, he appeared more annoyed than scared by the huge monster with the gun.

Everyone in the bank cringed, some of them covering their heads with their hands while they waited. Confused amazement crept into Ted's mind. He was certain that the man with the gun would shoot Mr. Willis – but he did not. He did not demand that Willis lay on the floor either. The two huge men just stood there, toe to toe, posturing like a couple of arched-back, puffed up tom cats squaring off to

5

fight.  The gunman began to loudly huff through flared nostrils beneath his ski mask.  The snorts of rage became louder and more terrifying with each breath.  The only ones who did not appear to be terrified, were the two imposing figures, angry and defiant in their standoff.

A large puddle of urine from the tuck-tailed man on the floor to Ted's left, made its way over, and warmly soaked into Ted's tee shirt as they lay there for what felt like forever.  In an eerily calm voice, Willis said to the man, "You can take that bag and just leave now.  You don't want to hurt anyone."  Ted was hoping and praying that Mr. Willis would just shut up and the man would leave before another customer walked through the door into this nightmare.

The man puffed his chest, and stood so close to Willis, that the hot fog of moisture, billowing through his knit mask as he shouted, fogged Willis' glasses.  "You're not callin' the shots today.  I am!"  He took his eyes off Willis and started looking around the room.  His agitation was clearly building, like a cornered dog that does not want to bite, but sees no other option.  "Ticka, ticka, ticka."  He murmured under his breath, and then, as if to scold himself, he shouted "NO!"  He turned an angry glare back to Willis as he walked over and stood above Sandy.  "Get up girl!"  He demanded.

# OMINOUS WHISPERS

Sandy was shaking, too gripped by terror to cry or scream, she locked her eyes on Ted's as she stood up.

"No, please!" Ted begged.

"Shut the fuck up!" the gunman said, kicking Ted in the face hard. His nose and mouth filled with blood, and a noise like a thousand buzzing hornets filled his ears.

"Come on now! You don't need to do this!" Willis pleaded with the man.

"You don't have a clue what I need!" The gunman bellowed back at Willis. He had Sandy by the hair, practically lifting her off the ground with his right hand. He had the bag of money over his right shoulder, and the shotgun held up, aimed toward her head with his left hand. "Everyone stay down for ten minutes. If anyone chases me, the girl dies!" It was the last thing he said as forced Sandy to leave the bank with him.

\*\*\*

Billy Kowalski had not heard the news about the bank robbery and kidnapping that occurred earlier that day, just a mile from his house. He was in his front yard, practically running as he pushed the lawn mower along the last stretch of uncut grass. He knew that if the grass was not done before his father got home, there would be hell to pay. Billy was not in the mood to feel or smell the tiny droplets

7

of spittle that would pelt his face, and go in his eyes, mouth and nose as they spewed, reeking of beer and rotting teeth, from his father's mouth as he screamed at him. Billy knew that neither truth nor lie would matter, one more than the other, as to the reason for waiting till the last minute to cut the grass. Truth was that he was doing it last minute because he was at the arcade all day trying to get his name as the high score on Asteroids.

Billy had long since given up on telling stories and lies to lessen his father's venom. For the past seven or so years, since he was about ten, Billy realized that the only thing that his father found satisfying, was to get drunk, and release all of his pent up anger on his wife and son by yelling, belittling, and beating them. His family knew this. Hell, the entire neighborhood knew it. Billy and his mother also knew, or maybe were simply conditioned to understand, that the only way to keep the rants and rages from going on all night, was to thank him for "caring enough to explain" things to them, to apologize for being stupid, and to recognize how hard it must be for him to be so smart and to be surrounded by people all day long, at work and at home, who were so stupid. Billy knew the nauseating script well. What he could not understand was if his father really was so fucked in the head that he believed that this lip service was actual respect from his family, or if he was simply satisfied that he could dominate something in his otherwise worthless life. Either way, Billy realized the futility of words long ago.

As Billy had just finished, and was rushing the lawn mower back to the garage, Ted's gold 1970 El Camino came flying up the driveway right behind him, squealing tires and bottoming out on the slope of the driveway, practically ripping the muffler off. "Damn it Ted! I nearly shit my pants!" Billy hollered.

Ted jumped out of the car, winded, sweaty and shaking as if he had run there instead of driven. "Billy! Shit man, I need your help!" Ted leaned forward and put his head down and his hands on his bent knees to calm himself and catch his breath.

"What's wrong?" Billy asked. He knew it had to be bad, because Ted was the most unflappable guy he knew. But now here he was, white as a ghost, with his front teeth missing and his upper lip and cheek swollen and full of stitches.

Ted gushed out the story to Billy, rapid fire, without a break for air. "Oh fuck man." Ted's voice shook. "He took Sandy! I was at the bank. I was goin' in to see her when the fucker busts in with a gun and robs the place! He made everyone lay down except old man Willis. The way Willis looked at him, I knew it then Man, he knew 'em.

9

He knew who it was. The fucker was wearin' a ski mask, but I know he knew him anyway. He just let Willis stand there and get into his shit! He told the guy 'You don't need to do this', but that just pissed the fucker off cause then he shouted at the old man 'you don't know what I need! I'll show you! I'll show you what I need!' Then he grabbed Sandy up from the floor and forced her to go with him. I tried to stop him! I tried to stop him man, but he kicked me in the teeth before I could even get up!"

Billy was speechless. His mouth was agape as he stood, just listening to Ted spill it all out.

"The stupid fuck told everyone 'don't move for ten minutes, or I'll kill the girl'. He took off pulling Sandy along with him."

"Shit, Ted!" Billy said, trying to absorb his words.

"I wasn't about to wait no fuckin' ten minutes. I ran to the door. All I could see is that it was a green Chevy van. I couldn't make out the license plate. Old man Willis was yelling at me to lay back down. Then, people started yelling at him that we need to call the cops now, but one of the tellers was already on the phone with them."

"Did you tell the cops it was a green van, and that you think old man Willis knew who it was?" Billy asked.

10

## OMINOUS WHISPERS

"I told them about the green Chevy van, but I didn't say nothin' about Willis because I could hear him tellin' the cops he didn't recognize the guy, but he did. I know he did".

"That's crazy? He knows who robbed his bank and he ain't talkin'?" Billy said as he shook his head and raised his hands in disbelief.

"Yeah. That's exactly what I'm sayin'." Ted replied. "And ya know what? I think I know who he's protecting. Tonight, I wanna go to his house, just you and me. If I'm right, we're gonna get Sandy back."

"Wait a minute, Man! You got kicked in the head. You're not thinkin' right! What makes you think *you* know who it is? Not only that, but what makes you think he hasn't already killed her, and that he won't kill us?" Billy was beginning to shout as fear crept up the back of his neck.

"Shut the fuck up man! Don't say that! Don't say he killed her!" Ted lunged at Billy, knocking him down to the ground. Ted started to cry as he rolled off Billy.

As the boys picked themselves up from the grass, Billy's father came home from work, and tried to pull into the driveway. "You'd better pull that old rust bucket out of my driveway unless you wanna' be blocked in by my car till tomorrow." Mr. Kowalski hollered up the driveway to Ted.

Ted got into his car and pulled it into the street in front of the Kowalski house. Billy walked over and leaned on the open driver's side window. "Yeah, of course I'm with ya Ted," he said, despite the warning bells in his head that were rising to a deafening level. "Hold on a minute, let me go make an excuse to my mom why I gotta leave."

"No, no, not till dark". Ted interrupted. "My parents don't even know I'm here. The only reason that the doctor let me out of the hospital, was because I promised to stay in bed for a couple of days. Besides, I don't want that fucker to see us coming".

"Good…OK. That'll give me a chance to get my dad's gun. I'll grab it out of his nightstand while he's getting' plastered in front of the TV."

"Good idea" Ted replied. "I'll meet ya at the end of your block as soon as it's dark."

"Who is this fucker that you think has Sandy, anyway? Whose house are we goin' to, Ted?"

OMINOUS WHISPERS

PART I

CHAPTER 1

AUGUST 12, 1978 – 12 DAYS BEFORE THE BANK

ROBBERY

Billy crept down the creaky wooden stairs of his family's tiny bungalow as quietly as he could. In his dingy, hole-ridden tube socks, sneakers in hand, he avoided the creakiest of the stairs, as if he were dodging land mines. He prayed that he would get out of the house without running into his father. It was only nine o'clock on a

## TAMMY GACH

Saturday morning, but Rick Kowalski did not keep his drunken rampages on any sort of a schedule.

Billy turned the knob on the door at the bottom of the stairs. His lip turned up in a sneer of disgust as he looked at his hand, and then wiped it on his pants. The door knob was sticky with God knows what, and now it was on his hand, along with a chip of old paint that had flecked off. Despite his many attempts to keep that damn door from creaking by planning the wood and oiling the paint encrusted hinges, it still creaked when he opened it - this time and every time. "Shit," Billy muttered under his breath as he opened the door and stepped into the hallway just off the kitchen. The tip-toeing and creaking door did not matter. Both of his parents were awake and in the kitchen. The mere sight of them gave him a sick, churning pain in his gut.

His father, dressed in nothing but a pair of filthy, not so white briefs, was seated at the chrome and red linoleum kitchen table that had been pulled from someone's garbage almost eighteen years earlier, just before Billy was born. Rick Kowalski had a cigarette in one hand and a can of beer in the other. Typical. The only time that those huge, ham-sized hands were not holding a beer and a cigarette, was when he was hitting someone with them, but then again, he did not always put down the beer and cigarette to do that.

14

## OMINOUS WHISPERS

Billy's mother was at the kitchen sink, wearing a stained, thread-bare bathrobe. A cigarette with a long, ready to fall ash on it, dangled from the corner of her mouth. She was rummaging through the week old pile of dirty dishes to find a cup without mold in it for her morning coffee.

"Aw shit, Mom!" Billy said it out loud when she turned around. He did not give a rat's ass if his father heard him or not, because the heat of his anger was welling up inside of him like a pot on the stove, ready to boil. Mary Kowalski's left eye was bruised and swollen shut. Her other eyebrow, the only one not too swollen to move, wrinkled down in a furrow of confusion, and her mouth fell slightly open, with the cigarette stuck to her lower lip. *It figures*, Billy thought. *She probably doesn't even know that she has another new shiner.* His mother lived her life in a drunken, perpetually battered haze. It is the only way he had ever known her.

"It's none of your God-dammed business you little prick!" Rick shot up from the kitchen table, knocking over the chair, sending its frame in one direction, and its old cracked vinyl seat in another. He slammed his beer can on the table, and strings of greasy blonde hair fell in front of his blood-shot eyes as he stumbled toward Billy. Billy clenched his fist in anger so hard that he thought his fingers might break. He wanted so badly to knock his father's

15

remaining, rotting green teeth right down his throat, but he knew that if he did, he would have to kill him. Pissing off his father was like jabbing at a grizzly bear that was high on PCP. His anger would not be quelled until he hurt someone - badly. Billy ran out the side door of the house, and down the street toward Ted's house six blocks away.

"That's right! Run – pussy – run!" Rick Kowalski hollered down the street, as he stood on his front lawn, wearing nothing but those stained, holey underwear.

Tears of frustration and hatred streamed down Billy's face as he ran. His father was not chasing him, but he ran fast and he ran hard anyway. He wanted to outrun his life. His heart was pounding like a jack hammer, and he hoped, for a moment, that it would simply explode and put an end to the pain.

Billy stopped running in front of Percy's Drug Store, which was half-way between his house and Ted's. He sat down on a cement parking block, at the far end of the store, to catch his breath. He did not want to look like he had been crying when he got to Ted's. He knew that Ted and his parents were aware of how rough his home life was. He also knew that Ted's parents would adopt him in a heartbeat if they could, just to get him out of there, but on the occasions when they did step in, it only served to make Rick angrier, and Billy's beatings worse. So, Billy decided to put on a brave face in front of the Greer's, for their sake, because he loved them. He loved them the way a son should love his parents, the way he never had felt for his own parents.

He lifted up the bottom of his marled blue t-shirt and wiped his face and runny nose on the underside of it, then walked into the store. "Hey Billy, how's it going?" Mr. Percy asked with his warm, gap-tooth smile that Billy had known for as long as he could remember.

"Can't complain Mr. Percy. Can't complain."

Mr. Percy, the store's owner and only pharmacist, knew that he would hear the same reply that he heard every time that he asked Billy how he was doing. Mr. Percy held on to the hope, however, that one day Billy would say "Oh, I'm doing great!" instead of "Can't complain." Mr. Percy, like everyone else in Warren, knew that Billy had a lot to complain about.

"Can I help you find anything, son?"

"Naw, just gonna grab a pop and chips I think. Thanks though."

Billy walked down the aisle where the travel sized toiletries were located on his way to the beverage cooler. He looked around, saw no one looking, and stuffed a travel toothbrush and toothpaste into his front pants pocket. He closed his eyes for a moment, and pictured his father's blackened, decaying teeth. He could almost smell the stench of rotting gum tissue as he tightly gripped the stolen toiletries in his pocket. Billy took a deep cleansing breath. *I will NEVER be anything like that disgusting prick.* He thought, as he opened his eyes. He felt lighter, like he had just taken a heavy backpack off his shoulders. He grabbed a Vernor's Ginger Ale out of the cooler, and a bag of Better Made potato chips from the rack, paid for them and continued on to Ted's house.

"He did it again, Mr. Percy. He shoplifted." The cashier shook his head in disbelief. The slight snarl on one corner of his upper lip, quivered with overt disgust.

"I know, Bob. But like I told you before, the only thing that he ever takes is oral hygiene products. I would give them to him if I didn't think it would embarrass him. For whatever reason, doing that helps him, and that poor kid needs some help, so please, let it go."

Billy was not stupid, and he knew that Mr. Percy was not either. There was no way that he could steal oral hygiene products from Mr. Percy's store, for six years, without being spotted at least a few times. Billy had quite the collection of tooth brushes, tooth paste, and floss; far more than he could use himself. He had long since stopped

18

feeling guilty about stealing. He consoled himself with the thought that one day, he would be like Robin Hood, and take the excess toiletries down to a homeless shelter in Detroit. He imagined that sample size items would be more practical for homeless people who lived a nomadic existence.

TAMMY GACH

CHAPTER 2

In a different part of the same town, Tom Willis, who was just a couple years older than Billy, was living his own special brand of hell.

*"Ticka, ticka, ticka, ticka, ticka"* Tom said quietly as he ran his fingers softly along the smooth, hand carved mahogany panels which separated the piano room of his family home from the living room.

*"Now, now, Tom. Not out loud"*, the beautifully smooth wood whispered to him as he caressed it. *"You know that your mother hates the ticka, ticka, ticka."* Tom knew that the whispers of the house were right, and he appreciated the reminder because he did not want to upset

20

his mother. He would rather dive into a pit of vipers, than upset that crazy bitch.

Tom found himself foolishly hoping that his father would be home tonight. Not that he had any use for the selfish prick, but he was getting tired of having to *comfort* his mother every time the bastard stayed away all night – which was nearly every night. *That's his fucking job, not mine!* Tom fumed. *So he better fix this thing with mother before I fix him!*

As he lumbered up the stairs to his bedroom, the sound – that damned sound - made him stop in his enormous tracks. His self-righteous anger instantly turned to an eerily subdued combination of dread, guilt and sexual arousal. He heard the bath water being turned on across the hall from his bedroom, and he knew right then and there that *Daddy* would not be home tonight. The sound of the running water triggered a sickening jumble of thoughts and emotions that he could not control - as if he were one of Pavlov's dogs. The familiar ache that happened every time he heard that sound seized his groin like a vice, making his testicles suck so close to his body that they nearly became internal. At times, he considered cutting off *those* parts because they caused him pain. He wondered what it would be like to be a girl. He did not really know any girls, except his mother, and that was different – *or was it?* He was starting to wonder.

21

# TAMMY GACH

*Ticka, ticka, ticka. I could push her head under that water, and that would be the end of that. But I suppose it's more his fault than hers. Men are supposed to be stronger, so what does he expect will happen when he leaves her alone night after night. When I have a wife, that won't be me! No siree Bob!*

Barb Willis stuck her plump little pasty white hand in the bath water. *Good, hot enough to kill those nasty germs.* She turned and strode, erect and purposeful, across the bathroom floor toward Tom's room. The low, wide heels of her black pumps clopped across the mosaic tiles like a Clydesdale's hooves across cobblestone. She knocked on his door. She *hated* knocking on a door in her own house. This was *her* house. Not her son's, and not, *most certainly not*, her husband's. It had been in her family for generations. But, the knocking was a compromise. As if she *really* had to compromise. But, fair is fair. After all, she had promised Tom that she would knock first *if* he promised not to tell his father about the baths, or about the way that he *comforts her* through her marital woes.

Tom yanked his bedroom door open with a force that could have ripped it from its hinges. He pushed past his mother on his reluctant stomp to the bathroom, nearly knocking her short, rotund body to the ground.

"You control that attitude, Mr. Willis!"

# OMINOUS WHISPERS

He hated that she called him the same thing that she called his father: Mr. Willis. *Cold, fat little bitch. Ticka, ticka, ticka, ticka.* He thought, trying hard to ignore his pangs of guilt. He preferred anger. Anger and hatred comforted him almost as much as the ornate woodwork of the house comforted him.

The water was hot when he stepped in the tub. So hot that it seared at his nerve endings, causing his skin to feel paradoxically cold. It always was. He was getting to the point where he could almost ignore the pain. He had developed a sort of *shut off switch* in his mind. As a child, he used to dance and jump and cry as his skin turned blood red from the blistering heat of the water. Now he just turned the switch in his head, but sitting down in the scalding hot water still hurt like hell. The switch in his head did not work as well when the burning water hit the really sensitive parts.

Shock waves that felt like electricity, shot through his body. He clenched his jaw muscles so tightly that some of his teeth had chipped over the years. He wanted to pull her in the tub with him. *Ticka, ticka.* He wanted her to hurt and burn and drown. She smiled and sighed deeply, contentedly, every time she watched him lower himself into the bath that she had prepared for him.

23

# TAMMY GACH

*Men are filthy. Filthy in their deeds, and filthy from birth. You can't help that you were born a filthy male. The least I can do as a mother is to keep you clean.*

Barb Willis usually knelt down. Her fat dimpled knees crushed into the little foam pad meant to protect them from the hard floor. Today she went and got a chair instead. That was a first. She was getting old, and she was starting to feel it. She allowed Tom to wash his own hair, and most of his own body. Most of it except for the *important parts. The really filthy parts that need special attention because that is where the germs live.* It was a routine that he knew well. He could do it perfectly. Just the way she liked him to. He could do it in his sleep, and sometimes did. He stood in front of her, and lathered the parts where the germs live, with soap. She watched, and made sure that he rubbed until all the wrinkles of skin were smoothed and stretched out. *That's where the bacteria hide, you know.* Then he had to rinse the soap off, so she could check for bacteria and germs. Barb would then rub her pugged nose up and down the shaft of Tom's penis, and nuzzle it in to his scrotum, sniffing and tasting for germs. The disgusting lump of a woman, who looked like a ball of raw bread dough, festooned with brown moles and skin tags, would moan and grunt with wanton glee every time she *checked for germs, and helped keep her son clean.*

24

OMINOUS WHISPERS

CHAPTER 3

Billy cut across the Perov's front lawn at the corner of Ted's street. He felt the start of a smile forming at the corner of his mouth. *So many birds chirping. Everyone has a tree in their front yard on this street, and the street is smooth concrete. I wish my street was concrete, and not that shitty patchwork blacktop. Better yet, I wish...NO! STOP WISHING! It won't change anything.* Billy took a breath, so deep that it hurt his chest, as he walked up the driveway toward the front door of the Greer's well-maintained brick ranch style home. The morning air was thick with honeysuckle and lilac. *Too* thick almost. He knew to take a wide path around those bushes that lined one side of the driveway. *That's where the bees are. Right there, right next to that quince tree. What in the hell is a quince anyway?* These were the frivolous kind of thoughts that he had when he came to Ted's house, and that is what he craved. Simple, happy, frivolous thoughts. He craved them like a fat kid craves candy, and he always got them when he was there.

The front door was open, and Billy walked in. He could not remember the last time that he was expected to knock first, or even if he ever was expected to knock. Everyone was home, happy and going about their morning routine, even Ted's sister, Karen.

"Hey, Bill!" Ted's dad said without looking up from his newspaper.

"Hey, Mr. Greer." Billy replied on his way to the kitchen where he could see a plate of cookies on the table. They were simple, store-bought, vanilla sandwich cookies, but the fact that Mrs. Greer had thought enough about her family to set out cookies on a Saturday morning was pretty damn cool in Billy's mind.

Diane Greer was a tall, slender, but not skinny, woman in her late forties. She had a shock of pitch black wavy, above the shoulder length hair, with a thin streak of gray on one side in the front. She loved the look and would not dream of dying that gray patch. She enjoyed telling people that the gray in her hair was a gift from her children. She turned from her breakfast dishes at the sink, but before she could ask Billy if he had eaten breakfast, she saw the red in his eyes. He had been crying. *Those asshole parents of his were at it again.* "You're a tough kid. You're a GOOD kid Billy. NEVER, EVER FORGET THAT!" She whispered emphatically in his ear as she gave him a tight squeeze of a hug. Billy smiled with the corner of his mouth and nodded his head. He kept his eyes on the cookies, because if he looked at her, the huge lump in his throat would give way to tears.

Walt Greer came into the kitchen to refill his coffee cup at the same time Ted came up from the basement into the kitchen. "What are you boys doing today?"

"I dunno," came in unison from Ted and Billy. Diane looked at her husband of twenty-five years, and gave a simple, quick raise of her eyebrows. She didn't need words. They didn't need words. She was his best friend. He spoke her language, and she was saying *Billy's having a rough go of it, so maybe you could do something with the boys today to take his mind off of it.*

"Guys, I just had an idea. I was talking to Alfred Willis over at the bank yesterday, and he told me that he has a couple sets of golf clubs that have just been sitting around, unused for ten years. He told me to swing by his place

27

today if I had a chance and he'd give them to me. So, you guys wanna go to the driving range today?"

"Heck yeah!" Ted said, patting Billy on the shoulder. "Whataya say, Billy?"

"Count me in!"

"Ya know, Diane, one of those sets of clubs is a women's set. Willis can't get the ol' battle-axe…*ahem,* wife of the out of the house, let alone to the golf course, but *you,* on the other hand, my dear, know how to have fun…"

"Yeah, Mrs. Greer! Come on! Come with us!" Billy chimed in knowing that Diane Greer is powerless when she looks into his pleading, soulful eyes.

As if on cue, Karen, Ted's older sister came into the kitchen. Oblivious to the conversation, she was lost in her slightly off key singing of *Play That Funky Music* by Wild Cherry.

"I'll go if Karen goes." *I'm going to have fun with this!* Diane gave an evil little chuckle to herself. Karen would be going back to Michigan State University soon, for the fall semester, and her mother was determined to spend as much time with her as she could before she was gone again.

## OMINOUS WHISPERS

Karen stopped singing and looked around the kitchen as if she were just noticing that there were people in there other than herself. "Go where?" She said, raising an eyebrow.

"Driving range to hit some golf balls!" Ted answered his sister, standing up a bit straighter, puffing his chest, and displaying the smuggest grin that he could muster.

"Oh hell no! Are you people insane?" Karen studied each of their faces, still not sure if it was a joke.

"Aw, come on Karen!" Everyone joined in. Their encouragement was loud, jovial, and relentless.

"This is bogus...fine, I'll go! As long as we're back in time so I can to get ready for roller skating tonight." Not that she would have ever admitted to it, Karen really did want to spend as much time with her family as she could before going back to State. *Even* if it did mean golf.

Walt and Diane smiled for the entire fifteen minute drive to the Willis place on the other side of town. The three teens were in the back of the station wagon, leaning against the tailgate with their heads out the back window, talking and laughing, their hair blowing in the wind. Karen was starting to see her younger brother as a friend rather than an irritant. He was athletic and popular. Even most of her college friends thought that he was a *fox*. She could

29

see why they thought so. Ted was six foot three inches tall with broad shoulders and wavy blonde hair. She had always teased him that he was adopted from a Polish orphanage as a baby because everyone else in their family had black hair. Despite his parent's reassurances that she was just trying to get his goat, he believed her until he was in the fourth grade. But now Karen liked hanging around with him, especially when he would come visit her at MSU. They always had a great time in East Lansing, more like friends than brother and sister. Karen would have denied it till her death, but she especially liked it when Billy came along with Ted to visit her at college. She had a serious crush on Billy for a couple of years now. He had a smoldering, bad boy look about him, combined with a soft, deep voice and the bluest eyes that she had ever seen. The last time that he came with Ted to visit her, and they all got a little drunk, she wanted to grab him and stick her tongue down his throat. But the next morning, she was glad that she was too chicken. She would have been mortified if he did not feel the same way.

*He* felt the same way, and had for a long time. *She's outta my league*, he thought, and left it at that.

Walt turned off the road onto the nearly hidden gravel driveway. "I'm glad I could still find this place. I haven't been out here in quite a while." Other than an unoccupied guard shack and an open wrought iron gateway, about forty feet up the driveway from the main road, all that could be seen was the gravel driveway, which was flanked by thick woods on either side.

After what seemed like several miles, there it was. Boom. Right in front of them as if it had suddenly come out of nowhere. Knob Hill, the residence of the Willis family.

"Whoa! That's the biggest house I've ever seen in my life! Ted stared, wide eyed, at the massive stone Tudor. Walt pulled the car near the front door along the circular driveway, got out and rang the bell while the others waited in the car.

"This place is creepy! Is *this* the house on the edge of town that I hear some kids say is haunted?" Billy asked Karen. He expected that she would know. She knew everything about that kind of stuff.

"You're so gullible! It's not haunted, it's just that freaks live here. Look, there's one now." Karen nodded her head toward the west end of the house.

"Karen, try to be a little nice..." Diane was starting to say as she looked and saw Tom Willis lumbering toward the car. He *was* pretty freaky looking, Diane admitted to herself. If he would have had an ax in one hand, and a head in the other, it would have completed the image. Tom

31

got about ten feet from the car, and then just stopped, stood there and stared at them. Knowing that his sister's typical response to intimidation was to throw it back at the perpetrator ten-fold, Ted jumped out of the car to greet the hulking, angry looking figure before Karen decided to get out and start running her mouth at him.

Ted stuck his hand out toward Tom for a handshake. After a brief, awkward moment, it became clear that Tom had no intention of reciprocating the gesture. "Hey there! My name's Ted. My dad came to pick up some golf clubs."

"You better go. My mother does NOT like to have people around." Flat, and as cold as the dead of winter, it was the most monotone, deadpan voice that Ted had ever heard. He could feel the hairs on the back of his neck stand up. Without another word, Ted got back into the car.

Karen could see the goosebumps on her brother's forearms, and busted out laughing. "I told you guys that freaks live here!"

"Who the hell was that?"

"Ted! You watch that language! It's bad enough that Karen swears all the time, but now you too?" Diane scolded her son. She was getting a little edgy and hoped that Walt would just hurry up and get the clubs so that they could get out of there.

"That mutant is Tom. He's Willis's son." Karen said with a slightly evil grin on her face.

"I didn't know that Mr. Willis had a son." Ted Said.

"Me neither!" Billy added.

"Yep, that freak, and then a bastard one too!" Karen liked how Ted and Billy were hanging on her every word. She loved her role as the cool older sister who always seemed to know the craziest things.

"Karen! Seriously, that's enough! I didn't raise you to spread gossip!"

"Come on, Mom! You know it's true!"

Diane just took a deep sigh and shook her head. Yes. It was true.

"What? How old are they? Does the bastard one go to our school? I've never seen freaky Paul Bunion over there at our school." Ted rapidly fired his questions while gesturing toward Tom, who was still standing there, ten feet from the car, staring at them.

"Jumbo Psycho over there was in the same grade as me, but in first grade, in front of all the kids, he just got up one

33

day, took the class guinea pig of its cage, and twisted its head off. I can still remember the sound of that thing screaming when he grabbed it. It still grosses me out."

"No way!" Billy and Ted said in unison. They looked at Diane in the front seat, and waited for conformation of Karen's gruesome story.

Diane pulled air in through her nose until her lungs were full and burning. She released it loudly; the frustrated sigh of a mother who realizes that children get older, and cannot always be protected from the ugly realities of life. "Sadly, yes. That did happen. After that, he got kicked out of a number of private, expensive schools. When he was about ten years old, they just pulled him out of school entirely. Dad and I have often wondered if that's what finally drove Mrs. Willis over the edge. Well, that and the mistress her husband took up with. She hasn't come out of that house in years. Dad says that she's always been a little bit off in the head, but I remember her as being a lovely hostess. The parties that they threw in that mansion were the best."

"Holy crap!" Billy gave a little scoff of a laugh that came out as a snort, which broke the tension, and made everyone laugh. "I just think it's kinda funny that there's a family out there that's as least as fucked up as mine!"

"Oh, you kids and your language!" Diane said, suddenly feeling fortunate that her kids were normal, swearing teenagers and that she had a husband who loved her.

"Well what about the kid he had with the other woman?" Ted asked.

"You probably know him." Karen said. "Jeff Bane. He's a jock, like you. One grade below you guys, I think."

"Yeah, I don't know him, but I know *of* him. Great athlete." Ted squinted his eyes and cocked his head as he considered what he was hearing. "Seriously? Those two are related? They don't even look like they're of the same species," he said, only half-jokingly.

Walt came from the house carrying two bags of golf clubs. He walked in front of Tom as he headed to put the clubs in the trunk of the car. "Excuse me, son." He smiled at Tom, who just stood there, in the same spot, staring at them as they headed down the driveway toward the main road.

TAMMY GACH

# CHAPTER 4

Despite the summer heat, a cold wind stung the side of Tom's neck and the back of his ear like a whip from a tree branch. "Well, what was I supposed to do? You know how she gets!" Tom said aloud, as he turned to go back into the mansion. He loved it when the scrolled woodwork and the polished brass wall fixtures whispered softly in his ear. This was not one of those times.

*Hate and fear are cancers that grow and take over, grotesquely distorting the soul until all the good is gone and there's no turning back. Yes, Tom – I know how your mother gets. I also know that you don't want to be like her, so when I feel the cancer of evil creeping toward you, I have to be heard, and you have to feel.* The mansion hissed an icy breath in his ear.

Tom felt the irritating gnawing of guilt in his belly. The mansion was right – he should not have been rude to the people in the station wagon, even if their presence might upset his mother. He knew that the mansion – his soothing friend, the mansion – wanted nothing more than to shake off the heavy, dark cloak of its past. Pain, suffering, hatred and bigotry had touched and scarred nearly every salvaged piece of wood, marble, glass and brass, long before they were used to build the grand dwelling known as Knob Hill.

# CHAPTER 5

## AUGUST 13, 1978

A sudden wave of nausea took Sandy by surprise as she stood at the kitchen sink drying the last of the Sunday dinner dishes. *Dinner tasted fine*, she thought. She had made her mother's spaghetti recipe dozens of times before, and had never felt sick afterward. "Hey, Dad." Sandy turned and walked the few steps from the kitchen to the adjoining family room, where father was in his usual spot on the well-worn brown plaid couch.

38

"Yeah, hun?" He turned to her, a smile still on his face from something funny that had just happened on an episode of *The Hardy Boys Mysteries*.

"Are you feeling OK? I'm feeling a little queasy after dinner."

"Oh? No, honey. I feel fine. Maybe you're coming down with something. Go sit on the pot for a while." It was the same fatherly advice that Dave Crane had been giving his daughter ever since she was a little girl, whenever she complained about a stomach ailment.

"God, Dad! You're obsessed with the toilet." Sandy went back into the kitchen and looked out the window. The leaves were already starting to change to the fiery colors of autumn, on the huge maple tree that she used to climb as a child. Things were so much simpler back then. When she was a child, a summer day seemed to last an eternity. Lately, she felt as if time was moving so fast, that she could blink and miss an entire day.

It was not the spaghetti that was upsetting Sandy's stomach. She wished it was. It was that damned gnawing feeling in the pit of her gut that she got when she knew that she might make a wrong decision, and let her mother down. *Why did she have to die so young? If she were here, I could ask her advice. I would know what she expects of me, and then I wouldn't disappoint her.* It was always the same thoughts, but now they were plaguing her more often than ever. People did not understand. How could a dead woman expect anything from her daughter? Her dad understood – sometimes. Ted used to understand, but now he becomes annoyed, and says "Stop obsessing."

Sophie Crane's only child had been the light of her life. Her little Sandy was beautiful, and smart. "You are so smart!" Sophie would get down on her knees, and say to her daughter. "You are going to grow up, go to any college you want, and become anything you want!" Then she would smile and say, "I can't wait to see you take the world by storm!"

*Oh, Mom. I wish you could tell me. Should I take the world by storm, or should I stay here so Dad won't be all alone? He misses you so much!*

The thought of leaving her dad all alone, gave Sandy a pain that radiated through her chest, as if someone had plunged a rusty ice pick through her heart. Almost a decade later, she could still see the image of her father, as clearly as if it was yesterday. It still haunted Sandy to remember him, standing alone in the funeral home where his wife lie in a casket. He looked like a lost child, not knowing which way to turn. He had lost his guiding star.

# OMINOUS WHISPERS

The Crane's bought their home in 1958, shortly after they were married. The love and laughter of family and friends warmed their modest tri-level home. Neighbors loved the parties and get-togethers that the Cranes regularly hosted. On weekends, the fun and laughter would last late into the night. The neighborhood parents would bring the younger children along, already dressed in their pajamas, knowing that the little ones would fall asleep on the sleeping bags that Sophie put in the blanket fort in the living room, that she had waiting for them to play in.

After Sophie's funeral, the first time that Sandy and her dad were alone in that house, he looked around and said something that his young daughter was not meant to hear. "It feels different in here. The light and happiness of this place must have died with her."

Sandy hated the thought that the little bit of love and happiness that remained, could be extinguished entirely if she left him there alone. She went and sat down next to her dad on the couch, and gave him a bear hug.

Dave knew the look in Sandy's eyes; he had seen it plenty of times. It meant that she was missing her mother, and worrying about him, so he held his daughter, and gave her a kiss on the top of her head. "You worry too much, kiddo. Let me tell you something. I knew your mom better than anyone.  Probably even better than she knew herself. We were best friends our entire lives – childhood sweethearts, you know.  So, take it from me.  Mom loved you, and was *always* proud of you.  When you were a baby, you couldn't blow a bubble without her saying, "did you see that, David!  That's our girl!' " He cradled Sandy's face in his hands, and looked into her eyes.  "She would want you to take the world by storm."

Sandy nodded her head as a tear rolled down her cheek. *He understood.    I don't know how, but today he understood.*

OMINOUS WHISPERS

CHAPTER 6

AUGUST 14, 1978

After Saturday's crazy golf outing with his family, and
the guilt that he felt about the way he had been treating
Sandy, Ted was happy that it was Monday.  He had a
workout session scheduled with Sandy, and the thought of
spending time with her brought a twinkle to his eye.  The
high school fitness room was open on weekdays during the
summer, so the athletes could stay in shape, and prepare
for the upcoming season.  A good workout always made
him feel better.  Not only that, but he loved how Sandy's
demeanor changed when she worked out.  She was, by far,
the best female athlete at their school – hell, she was the

best female athlete in the entire district, and she knew it. Whether she was competing, practicing, or just plain staying in shape, she brimmed with confidence and euphoria. She was alive and radiant on those occasions – no worries, no stress, and no obsession with making her mother proud. It was then that Ted felt the most love for her.

Sandy was already there at the gym, bench pressing weights, when Ted arrived. He was not surprised. She kept herself in excellent physical shape, and he knew that she was looking forward to the upcoming school year's softball and track seasons, because she talked of little else.

A few students were mulling about the weight room when Ted walked in. Only two of them were working out, Sandy, the only girl there, and an athletic looking kid with pitch black hair. The rest were just standing around and talking. After saying hi to Sandy, and giving her a kiss, Ted turned his head, and took a good look at the tanned and muscular kid with the black hair, and wondered if that was Jeff Bane. Ted had only seen Jeff from a distance, but that shock of black hair was a dead giveaway.

Even though he and Karen had been talking about him, just two days earlier, Ted knew that it was not some freaky coincidence to see him there at the gym. He knew that Jeff was an up and coming pitcher on the varsity baseball team.

44

# OMINOUS WHISPERS

Ted's thoughts turned to the past Saturday, and how Tom had just stood there, huge and creepy, staring at the car. How two brothers, even half-brothers could be so different, he wondered. He shook his head, wanting to shake the disturbing thought right out of it. It did not matter to Ted whether they were brothers, or even if the rumors were true, or if they made up. He had heard that this kid, Jeff, was good. Almost as good of a pitcher as he was. *That* was reason enough to get to know this kid.

Before Ted could approach Jeff, Kip Avery, a soft bodied, mean tempered kid, who was cursed with muscles that seemed immune to the effects of obsessive weight lifting, walked over to the weight bench, and stood over Sandy.

"Hey Sandy, I hear that you're stronger than Tarzan. Where do you keep all that strength? Do you store it in those giant tits of yours?" Kip said, with an oafish laugh.

Ted knew that Sandy could handle herself, so he stood back, and waited for the carnage.

Sandy put the barbell on the rest, and sat up on the bench. "Why yes, Kippy. I do store all of my strength in my giant tits. But don't worry. I can see that your tits are starting to fill in nicely, so it won't be long until you're as strong as me!"

Laughter, clapping and cheers filled the weight room.

Kip stood, slack-jawed, for a moment. "Fuck off bitch!" Was all that he managed to say.

"Hey!" Jeff growled as Kip turned to leave. "You deserved that Kip!"

"Oh yeah?" Kip turned and walked up to Jeff.

"Fuckin' A, you did! And, she deserves an apology." Jeff said.

Kip's face was beet red, and his chin began to quiver. He clenched his hand into a fist, and started to pull it back. Kip could feel the knot in his throat intensify. He knew that he would bust out crying at any second if he did not go on the offensive.

Jeff looked at Kip's clenched fist, and smiled. He stepped toward Kip until he was towering over him, a mere inch away. Without breaking his smile, Jeff looked down at Kip and said, "Do it! I dare ya!"

"We're cool, we're cool. Sorry guys, sorry Sandy. I was just kiddin' around. Nothin' worth fightin' over." Kip said as he backed away.

Ted stuck out his hand to Jeff. "Hey, you're Jeff...Jeff Bane, right?

Cracking his gum between words, he said, "Yeah. I'm Jeff."

When he put his arm out to shake Ted's hand, Sandy couldn't help but notice the well-defined triceps ripple on the back of Jeff's arm. She caught herself staring. It was hard not to. His wavy, coal black hair, crystal blue eyes, and the whitest teeth she had ever seen, were a striking contrast against his tanned body.

She forced herself to look away, just in time, to avoid being caught, gawking at him like some sort of ill-mannered troglodyte.

"I'm Ted Greer, and this is my girlfriend, Sandy Crane." Ted said, smiling as he stepped closer to Sandy and put his arm around her.

"Nice to meet you Sandy!" His smile was genuine, and it surrounded his perfect teeth, like just the right frame can add something to an already beautiful painting. "I hope that I didn't over-step, or embarrass you by putting that idiot in his place. Not that you needed help. What you said was hilarious! I never could have come up with something that funny, as quick as you did!"

Sandy smiled, and hoped that her face wasn't turning red. "Yeah, that guy's an Ass." She said. "You might wanna watch your back for a while. He's kinda squirrely, and he hates it when someone gets the best of him."

"Good to know." Jeff said with a smile and a wink. "But I'm not too worried about a jerk like that."

If any other guy had winked at her like that, after she had just said something, it would have come across as condescending and sexist, but that was not the vibe she was getting from Jeff at all. She had only known him for a few minutes, but he seemed like one of those people that you are at ease with from the start, and feel like you've known them forever.

Jeff turned back to Ted, and said, "Glad I got to meet you, man. You're like a legend around here to us younger jocks. I hear that all the colleges are trying to recruit you!"

"I think I'll probably go to State. My sister's there, so I've had a chance to check it out. It's one hell of a campus! Besides, I've just about got Sandy convinced to apply to State. It'll save me a shit ton of gas money if I don't have to drive home, or somewhere else to see her!" Ted playfully waggled his eyebrows at Sandy.

She had not told Ted yet, but her talk with her dad over the weekend had put her mind at ease about going away to college. Sandy felt certain that her mom would have wholeheartedly wanted her to go to Michigan State

# OMINOUS WHISPERS

University, because it was a tradition in their family; a legacy that dated back to the early 1920's, when it was still called Michigan Agricultural College.

Everything seemed to be falling into place. Life was good, and Sandy was finally starting to realize how lucky she was. Her summer job at the bank paid well, so she had almost enough money saved to buy a car, good grades came easily to her, so she knew that she would get at least some scholarship money, and now it looked like she and Ted would be going to the same college.

She thought about their friend, Billy. He still had both of his parents, and he had it far worse than she did, having only one.

But, there was still something. Some tiny little thing biting at the back of her neck that just would not leave her alone. A precognition of something yet to come, that she could not quite put her finger on.

CHAPTER 7

AUGUST 22, 1978

Alfred Willis was seated behind his 1920's burled walnut desk, in an oversized, tufted leather chair, perusing some loan applications. Both the desk and the chair had been gifted to him by his late father-in-law when Willis took over the reins of the bank from him. Alfred jumped a little when his extension on his phone rang. *Too much coffee*, he thought. He picked up the phone.

# OMINOUS WHISPERS

"Mr. Willis, there's a call for you on line one. The gentleman won't give his name. He says it's a private matter. Should I tell him that you're not available?"

"Ahh...No. Thank you, Susan. I'll take the call." He hesitated. Normally, he would not take a call from someone not willing to give their name, but his eyes were going crossed from looking over so much paperwork. Taking a call might break the monotony.

He cleared the phlegm and cigar smoke from his throat with a loud retching sound, then he pushed the button for line one. "This is Alfred Willis. How may I help you?"

The caller hesitated for a moment. He knew that Willis was a big man. He had followed him for days, and the pictures turned out great, but he did not expect his voice to be so booming - so intimidating. He gulped another quick shot of courage from the vodka bottle that his parents kept behind the bar in their basement, and then he said, "Could be today, or could be tomorrow. Either way, the cat will be out of the bag. Nothin' personal against you, but that son of yours needs to learn to mind his own business." Click.

"Who is this? Hello...hello!" Willis slammed the phone down when he realized that the caller hung up. He could feel the heat rising under the shirt collar that was mostly buried between the rolls of fat on his neck. His beady bloodshot eyes darted around as his mind raced. *What cat? What bag? My son? Tom almost never leaves the house. He couldn't be talking about Jeff. No one but he and his mother know that I'm his father.* He took a deep breath and dabbed the sweat from his round face with a monogrammed handkerchief. *Had to be the wrong number, the wrong Mr. Willis,* he thought. The thought appeased him.

Alfred Willis was a master at avoiding the unpleasant. He wallowed in his position of authority, and his self-perceived importance, like a sow wallows in the cool mud on a hot summer day. His world was how he deemed it to be. The emperor had no clothes, and no one was foolish enough to tell him.

OMINOUS WHISPERS

CHAPTER 8

Sandy did not get up to see Ted to the door. She remained sprawled out on the couch, just as she had been when he kissed her goodbye, and called her lazybones. He needed to head home and finish the chores that he had been putting off. She *was* feeling lazy. She had not been to the gym since her workout, the week before, had been cut short by the drama with Kip. She smiled, still amused by her own quick wit. The new school year was just around the corner, and she knew that her verbal smack down of Kip and his *tits starting to fill in nicely*, would spread like wildfire. Everything at that school did. None of the skeletons liked to stay in the closet.

Sandy considered going to bed early, and skipping the shower entirely. From her position, she could see the deep divot at the far end of the couch, where her dad spent way too much time. Suddenly, she felt the need to get up and get moving.

She was happy that her dad was not home, working on making the couch divot even deeper. He was at a neighbor's house playing poker. He was entering the land of the living more often lately, and tonight, he was doing something that he loved. *He might just be OK when I go off to college next year*, Sandy thought. With a nod of satisfaction, she locked the door and turned the porch light on because she knew that it would probably be dark when her dad got home. Before she made it across the room, there was a knock on the door.

Assuming it was Ted coming back, Sandy opened the door with a flourish, ready to say "You miss me already!" She was surprised and a bit confused when she saw Jeff standing there, looking a little sheepish.

"I hope you don't mind that I stopped by...I guess I kinda just wanted someone to talk to." Jeff said in a soft voice, as he nervously scratched the back of his head.

## OMINOUS WHISPERS

*Oh boy*, Sandy thought. There were those arm muscles again, bulging and rippling as he stretched. Her heart rate and breathing became faster, and she hoped that she would not stutter or say something stupid. "No, I don't mind, but how did you know where I live?"

Jeff looked down at his feet, and said, "I hope you don't think I'm a creep or anything, but I knew that I really wanted to talk to you, so I sorta followed you after you left the gym last week."

He stopped staring at his feet, and looked at her face to gauge her reaction. The look in his eyes reminded her of the big eyed, sad puppy dog paintings that were popular when she was a young child. She had always hated those paintings, because they would tug at her heart. "If that was my puppy," she would tell her dad, "he would never be sad again."

Now, here was Jeff, standing at her door, and she felt that old, familiar heart tug, once again.

"No, I don't think you're a creep." Sandy said, before she could consider *what* she thought. The warmth of her smile put him at ease. She was just about to invite him in, but the little voice of reason in her head, stopped her. Sandy did not feel threatened by Jeff, at all - it was herself that she did not trust. "We've got a pretty nice patio out back. We can go sit back there and talk."

"Sure." Jeff said, relieved that she did not just tell him to get lost.

"Go through that gate on the side of the house." Sandy said, pointing to her left. "I'll get some matches to light the citronella candles. Helps keep the mosquitoes away. I'll meet you back there."

She ran to the bathroom to check her hair and face in the mirror. Her lip curled up in a sudden snarl of disgust. Sandy did not like the girl who was looking back at her in the mirror. She got a momentary glimpse into the soul of the girl. The face was her face. It was the same reflection that she saw every time she looked in the mirror, but this was the first time that she saw deeper, and she did not like what she was seeing. Sandy had always been hard on herself, striving to be the best person that she could be, but, at the moment, she was disappointed by the girl who had a sexual desire, for the boy waiting outside. A throbbing wet heat coursed through her crotch. The intensity was so primal, that she feared it might be beyond her control.

Sandy shook a threatening finger at the girl in the mirror. In a quiet, deeply angry voice, she said. "You love Ted, and you will not cheat on him!" Then she went to the kitchen, grabbed a pack of matches, and two bottles of pop. She took a deep breath, and then stepped out the back door to the patio.

# TAMMY GACH

## CHAPTER 9

Barbara set her Bloody Mary down on the Baccarat Crystal coaster that she kept on her mahogany Chippendale accent table. She knew that she was not supposed to drink while on her medications, but she would sooner give up the medications, than the vodka. *Besides*, Barbara thought, *psychiatrists shouldn't even be called doctors. The only thing that they have in common with other physicians, is to get as much money out of wealthy people as possible.*

She grunted as she strained to lift herself out of the worn, tapestry upholstered wing chair. She heard the sound of tires on the gravel driveway, and hoped that it was the mailman bringing the latest issue of Tiger Beat

Magazine. *Dr. Katz thinks that it's a magazine for teen aged girls, and that it's not healthy for a mature woman to look at such young men. That quack Katz, well...he's a man. He doesn't know what I know. I know that when boys become men, they are replaced by robots. They're no longer human. None of them think that I know their little secret. So arrogant! Hiding under that thin veil. That's how they control the world, and I've got them pegged.* Barbara's lip curled and quivered with disdain as she sank deeper into her hate filled delusions. *Teen aged girls, with their clown makeup and tight clothes, full of fairy tale fantasies that they will be loved. Idiots. Robots can't love. They're just designed to convince girls that they are human, so they can fulfill their carnal desires.*

Barbara waddled from the solace of her comfortable chair, to the front door. Stealthy was not a word that could ever be used to describe Barbara Willis. She clopped around her Knob Hill mansion in hard soled shoes that looked too small for her. The fat of her sickly white feet poured over the top of them like over filled muffin tins. She could hear herself breathe as she made her way across the marble foyer, to the mailbox, located just outside the front door. She was certain that no one, but she, could hear the noise coming from her throat as she strained to breathe. Tom could hear it. The resonating sound was embedded in his mind, like an earwig that crawled in through his ear

59

and burrowed to the center of his brain. It was worse at night when she was lying in bed. On more than one occasion, Tom had considered putting a pillow over her face as she slept, to silence the noise that sounded like a pack of pug dogs fighting.

Barbara gave a huff of indignation. No magazine. She was starting to believe that the mailman was in cahoots with that damned Dr. Katz. There was, however, a large Manila envelope addressed to her. No return address. *Maybe they're delivering magazines in envelopes now,* she thought, as she waddled and clopped back to her chair and her drink.

It took a moment for Barbara to take in what she was seeing. The large envelope contained photographs of Mr. Willis. *Her* Mr. Willis, with a petite, middle aged, attractive woman with black hair, and a young man with black hair. *Who are these people?* She wondered. Her wondering came to an end when she saw the last picture. The picture in which her Alfred was kissing the woman. The sight sent a pain all the way through her barrel chest, like a knife had been plunged into her back.

Barbara began accusing her husband of adultery before the ink was dry on their marriage license. At first, it was simply the insecurity of a homely, overweight new bride who was well aware that she would have died a spinster, had it not been for her family's wealth and power. Over the years, however, the accusation became one of Barbara's favorite tools of manipulation. She honed her varied psychopathic skills, and became very good at deflecting her own heinous flaws by keeping her family in a perpetual state of confused guilt. But now, here it was – the weapon of a sick mind – the very thing that she never really believed existed – very real, arriving at her own home to attack her.

She opened the envelope wide, to see if there were any more photos inside. There was not, but there was a piece of paper stuck to the inside of the envelope. She could feel her face turn red with seething anger, but she was not prepared for what she saw written on that paper. The shock hit her like a tidal wave. Her face and hands went numb, and for a moment, she thought that she was having a stroke. Written in black ink, in capital letters on a piece of spiral notebook paper, she read:

MRS.WILLIS,

IN CASE YOU DIDN'T KNOW,

YOUR HUSBAND HAS A SON

WITH ANOTHER WOMAN.

TAMMY GACH

CHAPTER 10

Alfred left the bank early. He wedged himself behind
the wheel of his Cadillac Eldorado, and sat for a moment
before turning the key. He could not stomach the thought
of going home to Barbara and Tom. He still felt a little
rattled by the phone call that he got earlier, from some
crazy person rambling about *his son*. So, the last thing he
was in the mood to do, was to deal with his insane wife.
*She's getting nuttier by the day*, he thought. He reflected
on her decline over the years, and the increasing severity
of her accusations and lies. *Does she honestly believe that
I'm embezzling from the bank, or that I'm trying to poison
her and Tom, or that I'm sleeping with all the tellers, or
that I'm a homosexual?* He wondered. A pang of guilt
crept into his mind. *Is it my fault that she's crazy? She*

*accuses me of being unfaithful, but that's the only accusation that's true.* He started the car when he realized that he was sweating, and needed the air conditioning.

Alfred thought back to a time when he and Barbara were happy. He liked to believe that he never would have started his affair with Liz, if things at home had stayed that way, but he chose to forget that his affair with Liz started before his marriage to Barbara started its nose dive. He did not like feeling guilt or shame, and altering his memory of events was a good way to avoid it.

After Tom was born, Barbara's moods became darker, and her thoughts more erratic and twisted. According to Alfred's late father-in-law, Barbara's mother had *gone mad* after Barbara was born too. One week before Barbara's fifth birthday, her mother took a swan dive off the mansion roof.

*Barbara's father was lucky*, Alfred thought. *Bye, bye crazy wife! Why can't I be that lucky?* he wondered. The thought of Barbara climbing to the roof made him snort out loud with laughter. It felt good to laugh, especially since it was at his wife's expense. So, the pot calling the kettle black, he let his mind wander to the ridiculous. *Maybe she'll just explode one day! She's getting so fat, keeping herself locked away in that huge mansion, curtains drawn, wallowing in her delusions, and eating and drinking herself to death. BOOM! Could happen.*

Alfred pulled into the driveway of the modest brick bungalow that he purchased for Liz Bane when she became pregnant with Jeff nearly seventeen years earlier. It was a far cry from Knob Hill, but what it lacked in grandeur, it more than made up for it in coziness. Liz kept it immaculate. Every summer, she planted petunias, marigolds, zinnias, and even sun flowers in both the front and back yards, and the lawn and hedges were neatly trimmed. And in the winter, she kept the driveway and sidewalk shoveled and free of snow. As a matter of fact, it was the third summer in a row that the property won the city's landscape beautification award.

Alfred thought about his Tudor mansion, on the other end of town, with its stained glass, Pewabic Pottery tiles, and slate roof. It was beautiful once, too. Not as warm and inviting, but certainly, stately and elegant. Liz's home was made beautiful by love and hospitality – two things that no longer existed at Knob Hill. Since the plague of evil, greed, and child abuse infected the mansion, it was no longer beautiful. Now, it looked as if it had grown out of the cold ground beneath it - Big and dark and lonely.

Barbara's grandfather, Simon Shatsworth, spared no expense when he had Knob Hill built in the late 1920's.

# OMINOUS WHISPERS

He toured castles, estates, and churches throughout Europe, and imported entire rooms of wood paneling, Tiffany stained glass, and other architectural treasures from around the world. It is even rumored that ornate brass and woodwork from a ghost ship that ran aground on a Trinidad beach, in perfect condition, without a soul on board, was used in the construction of Knob Hill. Despite Shatsworth's obsession with every detail in the building of his estate, he never really *loved* the mansion. He only loved himself and his money.

Since its completion, the people who have occupied Knob Hill, basked in the glory of living in such a grand house. It made them feel superior. They loved being envied, and they loved looking down upon others from their high rung on the class ladder. None of them, however, had ever loved the mansion itself. For the most part, the inhabitants had been nothing more than a pack of self-absorbed prigs, unable to appreciate the skill and craftsmanship that went into creating the ornate and beautiful "bones" of the structure. They simply indulged their greed and gluttony at each other's expense, haplessly leaving behind their residue of evil to seep in, contaminate the mansion's soul, and darken its aura.

Alfred could feel the pulses in his neck and temples beat harder and faster as he sat in his car in front of Liz's house, reflecting upon how it came to be, that his life was bought and paid for. In his youth, Alfred had been popular and aggressive. His aggressive nature was evident in sports, student government, and in making connections with people who could help him climb the ladder of wealth and power. Despite his aggressiveness in anything that involved winning, he more than made up for his brashness with charm. People liked him when they met him, and loved him once they got to know him. He was tall and athletic. His thick, wavy, jet black hair, his piercing blue eyes, and his beaming, white-toothed smile, attracted people, and his soft-spoken, calm demeanor made them feel at ease. But now, twenty five years later, he was cockled, obese, and weak-willed. He had sold his soul to Simon Shatsworth, Jr., back then, but the Shatsworths had taken more than his soul – they took everything that was inside him – everything that mattered. His "gutting" at the hands of his in-laws, reminded him of the beautifully painted Russian eggs that had the inside blown out through a tiny hole in each end of the shell. Nothing left on the inside, but the shell was so ornate that no one remembered, or cared about what had once been inside. Knowing that he allowed it in order to achieve his coveted wealth and power, caused a chill to run through Alfred's core, making the sweat on his body from the hot summer day, feel like it was turning to ice.

# OMINOUS WHISPERS

*I could be happy here*, Alfred told himself every time he went to his mistress's house. He may have even believed it on occasion. This was one of those occasions. He entered the house through the side door, which opened to the kitchen, or the basement, depending on which way you turned. Liz was at the stove, making dinner for Jeff and herself. Alfred took a deep breath through his nose. The aroma of the food that was being prepared, by the only woman that he had ever truly loved, smelled like he imagined home should smell like. The massive kitchen and dining room of Knob Hill, never smelled like home.

"Al! It's a good thing that you showed up when you did. I just put the pork chops in the oven. I'll throw in a couple more." Liz said with a smile that showed Alfred that she was truly happy to see him come through the door. Liz Bane was happy – not just contented that she had a house, a car, and a bank account that were provided by Alfred – but genuinely happy. She considered herself lucky.

She fell in love with Alfred, many years earlier, when he was still young, muscular and charming. She would have married him when she became pregnant with his child, had it not been for that one little detail – he was already married. Even twenty years later, every time that Liz looked at Alfred, she still saw the man that she fell in love with. They say that love is blind – at least that is what

Jeff would say to himself whenever he saw his doe-eyed mother doting on the man who he had grown to hate. Liz could not see, or did not want to see, that everything about Alfred had become soft and weak over the years. He was bold and confident when they first met – willing to take risks for the things that he wanted out of life. Jeff had never seen that side of his father. All he could see, was a corpulent pig dressed in a hand-tailored business suit. The way Jeff figured it - if you can't bring your dirty laundry out into the light, then maybe you shouldn't let your laundry get quite so dirty. Liz, however, believed that she knew Alfred on a deeper, more personal level than anyone else ever could, or ever had. She believed that she knew his heart. Liz did still love Alfred, and yes, she was blinded by it, but she was, most certainly, not stupid. She felt that her arrangement was better than being married. She had seen too many married couples become resentful of each other, each expecting more that they were getting, and giving less than what was fair. Alfred never expected anything more of her than to keep Jeffrey's paternity a secret.

"I should have called to tell you that I was coming. I'm sorry." Liz could tell by the look on Alfred's face, that he was feeling low.

# OMINOUS WHISPERS

"You don't have to apologize, and you don't have to call. You know that." Liz said, trying to make eye contact with him.

Alfred simply nodded his head, and continued to look down.

Liz hated seeing him so distraught. It was happening more frequently, and as much as she wanted to help him, she simply did not know how. With a gentle sigh of frustration, Liz took a bottle of wine from the rack, and poured two glasses. "Here honey, let's start with this, then you can tell me what's been getting you so down lately."

Alfred took his glass of wine. He smiled softly at Liz, and then he took his handkerchief out of his pocket to dry the tears that were welling up in his eyes, and the ever-present sweat from his brow. "I could be happy here, with you and Jeff. You know? Here in this house." He finally said, looking back down, to avoid eye contact.

Liz was not expecting this – anything - but not this. His utterance sounded more like a question, than a statement of fact. "You know, Al, if you're thinking of doing it for me, or for Jeff, you know that you don't have to. We're fine, and I know how much you love Knob Hill, and being president of the bank. You'll lose all of that if you leave."

Liz was right. He was property of the Shatsworths. He knew it from the start. Hell, he even signed the contract, with a smile on his face, and a glimmer of greed in his eye. The money, the bank presidency, Knob hill, were a payoff from Simon, Jr. for marrying his mentally disturbed daughter. The main condition of the contract was clear. If he divorced Barbara, he would lose everything – his job, his home, and every last penny.

Shatsworth Sr. had two children, Simon Jr., and a younger son, Ansley, who died in 1929, at the age of twenty-one. Ansley was not married, and had no children. Junior had a wife, Ilse, and a daughter, Barbara. With no sons to continue the banking business, and a daughter who was groomed to be a debutant, and nothing more, the Shatsworths were in need of someone who could keep the fortune in the family, and Alfred Willis fit that bill.

Simon Shatsworth, Sr. had been born to a family of modest means. Like his future grandson-in-law, Alfred, he was aggressive, well-liked, and determined to become wealthy. After college, he took a job as a junior executive at a large bank. He watched, studied, and listened in on the conversations of his superiors, and their wealthy clients. Simon knew that if they could make big money, he could too. All he needed was a blueprint. He needed to know how they did it, then simply duplicate it.

# OMINOUS WHISPERS

Simon heard the men say, time and again, that it was a bull market, and it was. The prosperity since the turn of the century, made it an especially good time to exert his aggressive nature in the stock market. Simon had only two problems – not enough money to buy sufficient amounts of stock, and not enough knowledge to know which companies to buy stocks in. His charm, and eaves dropping skills would prove to come in handy.

To save money, Simon gave up his modest apartment, and moved with his wife and their two young sons, back home to live with his widowed mother. His mother didn't ask him for money for rent or food. She worried that if she did, he would move out, and she would be lonely again. He knew how she felt, and he used it to his advantage by squirreling away all of his money, with no intention of offering her any of it. He also took on odd jobs in the late afternoon and evening, after his day's work at the bank.

Throughout the early nineteen-twenties, Simon Shatsworth had managed to invest every penny that he could save, beg, borrow and steal, into the stock market. Simon knew that it was now or never. He had been hearing whispers that the good times would not last forever, and he wanted to get in and get out of the market as quickly as possible. His first delve into the stock market, was based on insider information, before that kind of underhanded dealing became illegal. He heard one of the bankers tell his stockbroker friend that a particular small company was going to be sold to a large, prosperous company, and that he was going to make a fortune by buying stock in the company before it was sold. Simon bought as many shares as he could in these "sure thing" companies, and then watched as buying frenzies drove the stock prices through the roof. He watched the cheaters closely, and joined them as they bought cheap stocks, and then traded them to artificially raise their value. When people saw the movement, they jumped in, further elevating the value. He bought when the cheaters bought, and sold when the cheaters sold, making fortune after fortune while the un-savvy investors were left holding the bag after the value plummeted.

Banks were giving loans to people, to buy stock that they could not afford. The thing was, that the bankers knew when to completely pull out of the market. They saw the crash coming. Average citizens did not have that knowledge, so they lost everything. The crash of 1929 left the country in a decade long depression that the money men survived. Few others were so lucky.

By the time that the stock market hit its peak in August of 1929, Simon Shatsworth, Sr. was a multimillionaire. He celebrated by having a vast mansion, Knob Hill, built as a monument to his own hubris.

OMINOUS WHISPERS

# CHAPTER 11

Sandy rearranged the patio furniture. She did not care if it was obvious to Jeff, or not, that she was doing it to avoid sitting too close to him. She walked to the far end of the patio, took a chair from the outdoor dining set, and dragged it over to where Jeff was lounging, legs crossed and hands comfortably behind his head. She plopped down on the blue and white flowered cushion, feeling a sense of control from knowing that there was room for only one on a chair, but room for two on the lounge chair that Jeff occupied.

"So, what's up?" Sandy asked, hoping that she was giving off an air of ease rather than the awkwardness that she was really feeling.

"Nothing much...well...maybe not nothing." Jeff shifted in his seat, putting his feet on the ground, and his elbows on his knees as he ran his fingers nervously through his thick, wavy hair. He was surprised that he felt nervous. He rarely felt nervous around girls. But this girl was different. Not only was she a little older, but she was the whole enchilada. Strength, confidence, and intelligence, all packed into a killer hot body. "Well, I guess that when I met you at the gym, you seemed really cool, you know. Not all uppity like a lot of the girls at our school. I felt comfortable, like you would be somebody nice to hang out with."

Sandy smiled, and immediately felt the familiar heat of blood rushing to her face. She hoped that her tan hid the bashful shade of red. "Yeah, you seem pretty cool too." Sandy gave a chuckle, as if to say, you hit the nail on the head. "I know exactly what you mean. Those girls drive me absolutely ape shit crazy! They snub the people that they think are beneath them, which is most of the school, and then they turn around and talk behind the backs of the one's they're nice too!"

"Yep!" Jeff vigorously nodded his head in agreement.

"And don't even get me started on the guys! I have absolutely no friggin' idea what goes on in their testosterone-addled brains!" Sandy did a little backpedaling, hoping that she had not offended Jeff. "I should say, not all guys. You and Ted, and a few others don't act all moronic."

Jeff studied the flower pattern of his lounge chair to avoid eye contact. "So, you and Ted been together for a long time?" Jeff worried that he was pushing it a bit, but it was the perfect opportunity to ask.

"Yeah, a couple years now." Sandy said.

"So, it's pretty serious then?" Jeff silently scolded himself. *No more relationship questions, dumb ass. You'll look desperate!*

Sandy could tell by his fidgeting that Jeff was interested in more than just a talking relationship, but she did not see him as desperate. She saw him as dangerous. Dangerous, because she knew the damage that she could do to herself, and others, if she were to become powerless to resist him. After a quick search of her mind for an idea that would allow her to have both Ted and Jeff, with both of them being OK with it, she knew that it was a scenario that did not exist. She knew right then, that she had made the right move by sitting in a chair with room for only one. "Yeah, we're pretty serious. He's been wanting me to apply to MSU, so we can be together, but I was hesitant to leave my dad here alone. I haven't told Ted yet, but I talked to my dad, and he convinced me that I should go if it's what I want. So, it looks like that is what I'm gonna do."

"So, it's just you and your dad?" Jeff asked, hoping that the question wasn't too personal.

"Yeah, my mom died when I was still pretty young, and I don't have any brothers or sisters. How about you?"

Jeff raised his eye brows and nodded his head. "Well, that's a whole other messed up story."

Sandy was just about to say, you don't have to get into it if you're uncomfortable, but she just sat and waited. She really wanted to know his messed up story.

"Well, some people would call me a bastard, but I've never really liked that term. It makes it sound like it's the kid's fault for being born. I'm the result of an affair between my mom and a married guy. And, get this, he's still married to the same woman, and his affair with my mom is still going on! So, she's his mistress, I guess, is what you'd call her. He pays for our house and everything else. He calls me son, but he won't acknowledge me as his son, in public, because it would ruin his precious reputation. Oh, and I have a half-brother that I've never met, because supposedly, his mother doesn't know about me or my mom."

# OMINOUS WHISPERS

"Whoa! That is kinda fucked up!" Sandy quickly closed her mouth, as soon as she realized that her jaw was hanging open. She did not want Jeff to be embarrassed or to be sorry that he opened up to her, but she was intrigued and wanted to know more about his life. It was like a soap opera – the over the top drama grabs you, then you're hooked – you have to keep watching – you have to know how it ends. So, she had to ask, "Do you *want* to meet your half-brother?"

"Yeah, I really do, but I've always been afraid that I'd mess up my mom's life if I started digging too deep. But, ya know what? One of these days, I'm gonna get up the nerve to just show up at his big-ass house and introduce myself! I know where he lives, so it's just a matter of getting up the guts."

"I think you should!" Sandy said with a brisk nod of conviction. "I mean, you've got a life too, and so does your brother. So screw em'! The way I see it, being good to your family, trumps what people might think of you – and this guy, your father, clearly cares more about how people look at him, than he does about his family."

"Pretty and smart!" Jeff said with a smile, but in his head, he finished the sentence with: *and off limits.*

Deep in their conversation, Jeff's compliment almost blew right past Sandy. When she realized what he said, her cheeks turned a healthy shade of scarlet, but that did not stop her from asking him more questions. "So, he has two houses and two families? That's gotta get pretty expensive!"

"He can afford it." Jeff said with a dismissive wave of his hand. "He's a bank president, and he's on their board of directors too. But I guess the money's his wife's, or his wife's family's, or something like that. Anyway, he'll lose it all if he divorces her. So, you hit the nail on the head. His money and his reputation are more important to him than we are. I wish my mom could see it. For the life of me, I don't know what she sees in him, and why she puts up with him. If it was up to me, I'd be happy to never see his fat ass again. He swears that he loves my mom, and that he can't stand his wife. I don't know why she falls for his shit. I wish that she would send him packing back to his wife." Jeff shook his head and huffed. A look of disdain came over his face when he thought about all the nasty things that he has heard his father say, over the years, about his wife Barbara. "You wanna know what dear old dad calls his wife? *The Nut Job.* That's how he refers to her. Real nice guy, huh!"

"The Nut Job?" Sandy's ears perked. "I work part time at a bank, and I've heard my boss say Nut Job under his breath after he gets off the phone with his wife. You can't be talking about Alfred Willis?" Sandy's mouth dropped open again.

"I guess it is a small world. Yep, that's the old man. Daddy Dearest!"

"I didn't even know that Mr. Willis had one son, let alone two!" Sandy furled her brows, and stared at the ground for a moment. "My dad always spoke highly of him. My mom and her parents knew him and his parents. That's how I landed my summer job at the bank. I'm the only one he's ever hired that's been under eighteen years old." Sandy shook her head. "Wow, I never would have guessed! At work he seems so nice."

Jeff shrugged his shoulders, and then downed his entire bottle of pop in four huge gulps. A belch of earth shattering proportions, burst from his mouth before he had a chance to stop it. "Sorry," was all that he could say before they both busted out laughing.

"Don't be sorry, that was stellar!" Sandy got up from her chair, and sat down on the lounge chair that was next to Jeff's. They were almost knee to knee sitting across from each other. Sandy felt a connection to Jeff – a connection that was deeper than the simple lust that she had been feeling – it was one of admiration and the desire to build a true friendship with him.

"I don't know if I shoulda laid all that on you, but you know what? I feel better! I've never told anyone about my family. Just you. It's not that people don't know, hell, I bet that half of the kids in school know. It's just that I've never talked about it until I told you."

Sandy could see big alligator tears welling up in Jeff's crystal blue eyes. She jumped up before one of the tears rolled down his face. "How about another bottle of pop? Maybe you can give a repeat performance of the burp to end all burps!" She said as she turned around and headed for the house. She wanted to save him the embarrassment of her seeing him wipe his tears.

Jeff knew what she was doing, and he was grateful. It confirmed that his first impression of Sandy was spot-on. Sandy Crane was, indeed, very cool.

"Sure, another one would be great, but a beer would be better!" He said as he quickly dried his eyes on the same part of his shirt, where he had earlier wiped his mouth.

"Ah...I think my dad has some beer in the fridge."

# OMINOUS WHISPERS

"No, I'm kidding! I can't be getting all liquored up. You might take advantage of me!" Jeff joked, having no idea how close he was to the truth.

They talked and laughed for another hour, but they could have gone on all night. It was easy conversation – comfortable, like they had known each other forever.

"I better head home. I'm sure that my dinner's cold, and my mom's temper is hot by now!"

"OK, well, I'm glad that you stopped by. It was a really nice conversation. We should do it again." Wanting to see Jeff again, even if only as friends, triggered a dilemma. "Ah, Jeff...I hope that you don't think that I'm a jerk, but I don't think that either of us should mention this to Ted. I'm just not sure that he'd understand, and I don't want him to get jealous or angry over nothing. OK?"

"Oh, yeah. No, I wasn't planning on saying anything." As he walked home, Jeff thought about the phrase that she used – *over nothing*. It stung a little to think that she thought of him as nothing, but he did not really believe that. He was something. She was something. There was something.

# CHAPTER 12

Jeff smiled all the way home from Sandy's house – that is, until he saw Alfred's car parked in front of the house. *Aarrgghh! Buzz kill!* He thought as he went inside.

"Why so late?" His mother pointed at the clock on the kitchen wall.

"Hi, Jeff." Alfred chimed in.

Without acknowledging Alfred's greeting, Jeff looked at his mother with the same puppy dog eyes that had warmed Sandy's heart earlier that day. "Sorry Mom. I made a couple of new friends, so I stopped to talk with one of them, at her house, for a while. I didn't think that we had talked for very long, but I guess we did."

## OMINOUS WHISPERS

"Her, huh? Were her parents at home?"

"No, Mom. They weren't but, I didn't even go inside the house. We sat outside – and just talked."

"What's her name?" His mother asked with a smile.

"Sandy Crane."

Alfred's huge, round head nearly spun off his shoulders, he whipped it around so fast.

"Yes, Alfred. I know. She works at your bank." Jeff didn't even try to hide his disgust at Alfred's reaction. He knew that his father's squirming little brain was going into its usual self-preservation mode, and that his mother would coddle him until he was back on his pedestal, assured that he was not a selfish man. It was the same nauseous scenario that played over and over again.

Like a reward conditioned lab rat, Liz grabbed another bottle of wine from the rack. She had it opened, and Alfred's glass refilled before he could formulate a way to ask Jeff if he told Sandy about his paternity.

"You didn't tell her, did you?" Alfred, hesitantly asked. The fat of his jowls began to quiver with nerves.

Jeff wanted to toy with him, and let the nervous pressure build until this sad excuse for a father of his, popped an artery in his head. Jeff sat next to Alfred, at the small kitchen table, and looked him square in the eye. "Are you really delusional enough to believe that no one, other that the three of us in this room, knows that I'm the shame that you carry around with you day in and day out, but hide so well? The bastard son who could ruin it all for you – your wealth, your position at the bank, your oh-so-important status in the community. Well, news flash, *Dad* – most of the kids at school already know. They've been harassing me about it since the seventh grade. And I can't *imagine* how the kids found out – their parents, maybe?"

Alfred's face was as red as a steamed lobster. Both he and Liz were too flabbergasted for words. Alfred was mortified by the thought that he had been walking around for years, blissfully ignorant, while the entire town laughed at him behind his back. And, Liz felt the crushing weight of guilt that had just hit her. How could she not know that her son had been silently burying the pain of ridicule for years? She was so busy enjoying the easy life that Alfred provided for her, that she ignored her son's growing resentment of him.

I'm gonna skip dinner tonight, Mom. I think I'll listen to some music in my room, then go to bed." Before he left the kitchen, Jeff looked at Alfred and said, "Seems to me that, the family you have stashed away in that ice palace mansion, on the other end of town, may be the only ones who are still in the dark."

A storm of rage seethed within Alfred. He felt like punching Jeff for destroying his fool's paradise, while Liz was simply embarrassed by her son's disrespectful outburst.

As blindsided as Alfred and Liz were, deep down, they knew that it was their own doing that got them to this point. There was no sand to bury their heads in tonight.

Alfred scrunched his eyebrows in momentary confusion, and then put his head in his hands when he thought about the mystery phone call that he got at the bank earlier. He lifted his tear stained face, and gently held Liz's hands. "I got a phone call at the bank today. At first I figured that it was a wrong number, that he called the wrong Alfred Willis. Now, I'm not so sure. My life is crashing, Liz. It's all crashing down on me." Alfred began to sob.

"What phone call, Al?" Liz wiped away his tears with a kitchen towel, then grabbed a package of his favorite cookies out of the pantry.

He stuffed three cookies in his mouth. Unable to restrain his need to unload his concerns on to someone else, he sprayed crumbs across the table as he talked. "A man called and said the cat was going to be let out of the bag today or tomorrow, or something to that effect. Then he said it wasn't personal against me, but my son should mind his own business. My son, Liz! People do know, and now they're trying to ruin me! That little prick has probably been going around telling everyone that I'm his father, because he hates me and wants to ruin me!"

"What!" Liz shouted. "You better not mean Jeff!" Her eyes glared at him.

Alfred recoiled. A wad of half chewed cookies fell out of his mouth when his jaw dropped open. Liz had never raised her voice to him before. It suddenly sank in that she had never done anything except show him love and devotion, for the past twenty years. A better man would have felt shame for using such a loving woman as his emotional dumping ground, and allowing his son to be treated like a second class citizen. But no, not Alfred. He tried to back-pedal. "No, honey. Not Jeff." He lied. "I would never call Jeff a prick – or any bad name, for that matter. I don't know. I don't know what I'm thinking."

Liz did not entirely believe him, but she did what she always did – pamper him and convince him that everything was going to be fine. It's the only job that she ever had, and she was very good at it. "You stay here with me tonight, my Sweetie-Bear. The last thing you need is to go home and deal with *Nut Job*, when you've already had a very stressful day."

Alfred nodded his head, and stuck out his lower lip in the kind of pout that is usually reserved for two-year-olds. Liz held his head against her body for a moment, then she poured him another glass of wine.

## CHAPTER 13

A Jim Croche song played through his stereo headphones as he flopped down on his bed and tried to unwind. Music could usually relax Jeff. He loved to get swept away on a magic carpet of rhythm and melody, and completely lose himself in the music. Tonight was different. He had never been *verbally* disrespectful to his father. Make no mistake, it was crystal clear to both of Jeff's parents that he did not have even the tiniest grain of respect for Alfred Willis. He had shown his disdain for him, over the years, by ignoring him, pretending that he couldn't hear him, or simply by giving him a dirty look when he felt he could get away with it. But he had never said what he had been feeling ever since he was old enough to know what "bastard kid" meant. He thought that speaking his mind would be liberating – and it might have been – if that was all he needed.

Jeff realized that it was not because he spoke his mind to his father, that he could not relax, it was that he could not stop thinking about his conversation with Sandy. *You've got a life and so does your brother*, was playing over and over again in his head, louder than the music through his headphones. Sandy was right. It was just going to keep irritating him like an incessant little dog, nipping at his ankles, until he put himself first for a change, and went to meet his brother.

Jeff took off his headphones, turned off his stereo, and waited for the, all-too-familiar, nausea-inducing sound. After about twenty minutes, he heard it, coming from across the hall, in his mother's bedroom. It was the appalling sound of the bedsprings, screaming under the heft of his father, as he wallowed and flopped in bed, trying to find a comfortable position for his many rolls of fat. Before long, Alfred was snoring like a glutted walrus. Jeff left his bedroom, and quietly made his way to the living room. He was happy when he looked out the window, and was reminded that Alfred's car was parked in the street, rather than in the narrow driveway, which would have blocked in Liz's car. *It's a good omen!* Jeff thought as he gently lifted his mom's car keys from the little ceramic bowl on the counter, near the back door. His heart raced as he put the white Mercedes into neutral, and pushed it down the driveway and into the street. *That was as easy as it looks in the movies!* He laughed to himself. Convinced that he was likely out of his mother's ear shot, he started the car. For a moment, he thought about going to get Sandy. The magnitude of what he was doing, was starting to set in. He was stealing his mom's car, driving to the house where Alfred's wife lives, and where Alfred is supposed to be living, and meeting a guy, who may or may not be happy to find out that he has a half-brother. But, as much as he could use more encouragement from Sandy, and would love to have her company, Jeff knew that he just needed to buck up and go do it on his own.

OMINOUS WHISPERS

CHAPTER 14

The sour taste of stomach acid crept up the back of Barbara's throat, and burnt her tongue. She fought a strong urge to vomit when she forced herself to take a good look at the young man who was in one of the pictures that, so cruelly, had been sent to her. Barbara squinted to focus. Her pudgy hands began to tremble and her brightly painted red lip raised at the corner in a snarl of anger as she stared at the spitting image of a young Alfred Willis. A modern, taunting version of the Mr. Willis who vowed to *forsake all others, and remain faithful to her, until death do us part.*

Tom was shocked awake from his nap, by the sound of crashing glass, and his mother's howl. Her shriek of anguish sounded like something that might come from an animal having its leg crushed in a steel trap. He jumped up from his bed to go check on her, but he stopped in his tracks before he reached his bedroom door. *Mother may think I'm stupid, but I'm smart enough to stay away from her when she's angry. Ticka, ticka, ticka.* Tom started to pace, and chew on the jagged edges of what remained of his fingernails. He felt the pain shoot through his groin as his testicles cringed in anticipation of the sadistic, sexual assault that his mother often inflicted on him, to make herself feel better.

Tom clenched his fists and could hear his own breathing become faster and louder as he waited for the knock on his bedroom door. Instead, he heard his mother's bedroom door slam, then the repetitive sound of bed springs screeching in unison with the thud of her headboard as it slammed against the wall. He could hear his mother crying, swearing and talking to herself. He was grateful that he could not make out what she was ranting about, and even more grateful that he could not imagine what she was doing to cause her bed to slam against the wall.

Tom took comfort the only way that he knew how – by going down to the piano room and listening to the melodious, soothing sounds of the mansion as he, and the beautiful woodwork, engaged in intimate conversation.

# OMINOUS WHISPERS

After about an hour of successfully drowning out the sound of his mother's breakdown, Tom went to the foot of the staircase, then stopped to listen. He heard the sonorous rumble of his mother's snores, and realized that she had finally worn herself out. With a sigh of relief, he knew that he was safe, at least for a while. He went to his mother's sitting room, to see what the crash had been. The blood red remains of a spilled Bloody Mary, and shards of broken French crystal lie on the parquet wood floor between her favorite chair, and the stone fireplace where she had thrown her drink. Tom went to the maid's closet to get a broom and mop. He feared that if it was not thoroughly cleaned up by the time she came down from her room, she might be reminded of whatever had set her off, and she would go back into her rant.

After he cleaned the floor and the hearth, Tom turned his attention to his mother's chair and mahogany accent table. He replaced the crystal coaster that she kept there, with one from another table, and straightened her magazines. He picked up the photos that were strewn across the seat of her chair, and started to straighten them before putting them on the table. His head cocked to the left, and his eyebrows furled in confusion when he caught a glimpse of the people in the photos. The date printed on the corner of the pictures was, August/78, so they were recent. The only person he recognized was his father.

# TAMMY GACH

When Tom flipped to the picture of his father kissing a woman, he instantly knew the impetus of his mother's atomic meltdown.

Tom's hatred of his father surged and he could feel the blood course through his veins as if it were on fire. He did not care that his father had caused his mother pain – she deserved that. Hell, it would even be funny, if she would take her wrath out on the person who caused her pain, and not on him. But no, that was wishful thinking. Tom knew that he would take the hit. He hated his father for leaving him in the position to have to be his proxy, once again, for every disgusting, painful, sexual act, that his mother wanted to inflict upon her husband, but could not. Alfred Willis was perfectly willing to throw his embarrassment of a son, to the wolves, while he kept his own head buried in the sand, safe from all that was unpleasant.

Fear and anger were building in Tom's head, causing his temples to throb with pain. He started picking at his fingernails with his teeth again, until he chewed the one on his right middle finger, completely off. He had never seen his mother this angry before, and it was freaking him out. He knew that she would release her rage upon him, like always, but this time he expected that it would be a doozy. *Ticka, ticka, ticka,* played, like a broken record, through Tom's mind as he made his way back to the piano room. He needed soothing, so he began to run his fingers, lovingly, along the scrolls of the woodwork. The relief that he felt was immediate, sweet and intense. The beautiful, ornate scrolls of hand-carved wood were once again softly whispering to him.

*"There's evil emanating from her, Tom. It's penetrating the walls, the floors, everything – deeper and uglier than ever before. You should be outside today, Tom. Don't stay inside. You'll get trapped in the black, toxic fog that's leaching from her pores. It's roaming these halls, Tom, like the thick stench of a rotting corpse."* The ominous warning, delivered by the beautiful sound, suddenly stopped. Tom tried to get the soothing sound to come back, but not even his softest caress could coax the mansion to continue. The whispers wanted him out. The mansion did all that it could to protect him from his mother, and the vile hatred with which she adorned her home.

## CHAPTER 15

Jeff knew exactly where the unlit gravel driveway of his father's house was located. Since the day, a decade earlier, that Jeff's mother had explained to him that Alfred was his father, and his father had a wife and a son across town, Jeff imagined, in detail, going there to meet his brother. He studied the entrance to that driveway, every time that he and his mother drove past it, and now, here he was. Jeff could feel the goose bumps raising on his arms, and his peripheral vision narrow and darken in trepidation, as he drove up the long driveway. He stopped when he reached the part of the driveway that circled in front of the mansion. He put the car in park and turned off the headlights. He needed a moment to consider his options. You see, this was the part of the scenario that he had imagined a thousand times, with a thousand possible endings. With a deep breath, Jeff thought, *Hope for the best, but expect the worst.* Unable to come up with a better pep talk for himself, he sat for a moment longer, tapping his fingers on an imaginary piano keyboard on his knees, as he listened to the car radio, turned way down low.

*There's no other way*, Jeff decided. *I'll simply go and knock on the front door, and hope that a guy, around my own age, answers it instead of Nut Job.* He could see at least one light on upstairs, and one on the main level as well, so someone was probably still awake. He decided that he would leave the car running, just in case he was met with hostility. He looked down, wiped the sweat from his palms on his jeans, took a deep breath, and reached for the car door handle. His heart nearly jumped out of his chest when he looked up and saw a massive guy, as big as Alfred, but not as fat, lumbering toward his car.

Jeff's first reaction was to put the car in drive, whip it around, and take off. *Don't be a puss. You've waited ten years to do this. Don't back down now!* He told himself. He did not realize that he was holding his breath, as he rolled down the car window, until he felt light-headed and gasped for air. The man had to bend way down to see into the car. Jeff cleared his throat first, in fear that his voice would crack, then asked the giant, "Is Tom home?"

97

# TAMMY GACH

Tom stared at Jeff for a moment. No one had ever come to his house to see him. Not once, not ever. "I'm Tom," he said in a voice so meek that it not only surprised Jeff, but also helped put him at ease.

"Listen, man. I really don't know of a good way to say this. The whole thing is so fucked up that I just don't know what to expect from anything anymore." Jeff said, wiping even more sweat from his palms onto the front of his jeans.

Tom felt a rush of warmth flood through him that he had never felt before. He felt human. A guy – a guy about his own age, was talking to him. There was something about him - about his mannerisms that was pushing Tom's apprehension further and further into the background. Tom wanted to ask, Say what? But, his limited experience with people taught him that his social skills were virtually nonexistent, and he tended to scare people. So, he waited for the stranger in his driveway to explain.

Jeff looked down at his lap again, then he just spit it out. "I don't know if you know about me, or if this is going to come as a big surprise to you, but we're half-brothers."

Tom cocked his head to the side, like an intrigued dog hearing a whistle. He stood silently and stared, for what seemed like an eternity to Jeff.

# OMINOUS WHISPERS

"What do you mean – half-brothers?" Tom finally asked.

Jeff could see, by the look in Tom's eyes that his confusion was genuine, so he treaded lightly, and answered as delicately as he knew how. "Well, it turns out that you and I have the same father, but different mothers." Hoping to ease the shock, Jeff quickly added, "I really hope that you're not mad, but I really needed to meet you." The warm summer breeze felt cool when it hit Jeff's sweat-soaked shirt. "I mean, I would like to get to know you."

Tom thrust his hand through the open window of the car. Jeff gasped and his entire body cringed in reflex. He expected to be grabbed by the shirt and yanked from the car, but when he opened his eyes, he did not see a monster ready to devour him, he saw Tom, smiling from ear to ear, waiting for his brother to shake his hand. Feeling relieved, and a bit foolish, Jeff gave a nervous laugh, and shook Tom's massive hand.

"Good to meet you. My name's Jeff, by the way. You wanna come sit in the car and talk for a while?"

Jeff was surprised to see a guy so big, move so fast. Tom was in the car, knees cramped between the dashboard and his chest, smiling and eager to talk.

"I'm not mad. I'm happy!" Tom said. He scrunched his eyebrows. "I guess I don't understand. Does my father have two wives?"

"No, just one." Jeff was disturbed by the sight of Tom sitting all scrunched up, like one of a dozen clowns being packed into a tiny car. "Hey, why don't you reach down and pull the lever to move the seat back – give your legs a little more room."

"I know I'm big." Tom said, hanging his head as he moved the seat back.

The look of shame on Tom's face made Jeff's heart sink. "No, man. It's cool. Hell, if I was your size I could really kick some ass on the football field! Jeff smiled and patted Tom's shoulder. Like an about face, Tom's smile returned. He could not remember a time when someone had actually made him feel good about himself. Jeff knew that his answer to Tom's question wasn't sufficient, so he continued to explain. "Alfred is married to your mother, but not to mine. My mother is just his mistress. They have been having an affair for twenty years. I'm a product of that affair."

Tom's mouth hung open, and his right eyebrow was raised. Jeff didn't know if Tom was confused or surprised, or both. Tom closed his mouth and shook his head. "My mother has always accused him of having affairs, but I know that she never really believed that he was. She just likes to be mean." Tom suddenly stopped talking. He put his hand over his mouth, and gasped. "The pictures!" He said.

Now it was Jeff's turn to cock his head to the side in confusion. "What Pictures?"

"Oh, you don't know? I just thought, for a second, that maybe you sent them to my mother." Tom paused before he asked, "Does your mother have black hair?"

Still confused, Jeff answered in a tone that sounded more like a question. "Yeah."

"My mother got some pictures in the mail today! They were pictures of my father with a woman who had black hair. I think that you were even in one of the pictures!"

"Today?" Jeff's eyes opened wide. He was still confused. "So, you think that your mom found out about me and my mom today?"

"Yeah. She went bananas! I've never seen her so mad. She's been locked in her room all day, ranting and throwing shit around."

Jeff noticed that when Tom mentioned his mother's rant, he got a look of fear in his eyes like a dog expecting to get hit with a rolled up newspaper for peeing on the floor. "I've got no idea who would have pictures of us, let alone, send them to your mom. My mom and I have always been the dirty little secret that he tried to keep hidden." Jeff scratched his head. "Well, the old man musta pissed somebody off enough that they would want to really screw with him!"

Tom nodded, staring off into the distance, with the same fearful look in his eyes. Ashamed that she had so much power over him, he asked Jeff, "Is your mother crazy too?"

Jeff wanted to chuckle, but he could tell that Tom meant it to be a serious question. He didn't want Tom to think that he was laughing at him, so he smiled and said, "No, but sometimes she makes me wonder!" Jeff gave Tom another pat on the shoulder, and said, "Listen, why don't we exchange phone numbers. I've gotta get my mom's car home before she notices it missing."

Tom's face dropped as if it had suddenly melted. "Ok, but I should probably call you, because if my mother answers, I'll really pay for it."

Once again, Jeff could see that Tom was serious, but he had no idea how insanely vicious Barbara Willis could be. He could not have imagined that Tom would be so happy to meet him, and so sad that he had to leave. It was way better than any of the scenarios that he envisioned over the past decade. "I'll tell you what, I can come back on Friday – three days from now – around nine in the morning. My mom will be out with my Aunt all day, and they almost never take my mom's car. We can talk some more then, or maybe go do something. Sound good?"

"Better than good!" Tom beamed. "No one's ever come over to see me before! I'll be waiting outside, right here!"

Every bit of fear and uncertainty was erased from Jeff's mind. Now he knew that meeting his brother was the right thing to do, *and if anybody doesn't like it*, he thought, *well, they can just kiss my ass!*

Jeff racked his brain as he drove home, wondering who had pictures of his family, and what sleazy thing his father must have done to them, to get them to want to hurt him. *I would love to be a fly on the wall of that mansion when Ol' Alfred's crazy wife confronts him with those pictures!* Jeff thought. Then his blood ran cold. *Shit, I hope she doesn't kick him out! He'd move in with us, then he'd be there every night!*

Tom could not have cared less who sent the pictures. He was thrilled to have a brother – someone normal who

103

seemed to like him. Tom wanted to revel in glee. He had never felt so happy, but his happiness proved to be short-lived. His mother *would* get ahold of him, and it *would* be horrific.

As for Kip Avery? Well, how could he possibly know that sending those pictures would ruin so many lives, and that the one person who he had wanted to suffer, Jeff Bane, would escape – the least scathed of all.

OMINOUS WHISPERS

CHAPTER 16

AUGUST 23, 1978

Barbara Willis woke up with her face, and the clumps of hair that she had ripped from her own skull, stuck to a drying puddle of drool and tears on her pillow. Worn out by her hysteria, she did not realize until she looked at the clock, that she had dozed off for most of the day. And she certainly did not realize that just an hour earlier her husband's bastard son was in her driveway making friends with Tom.

It would not have mattered. There comes a point when a fire just cannot get any hotter, no matter how much gasoline is poured on it. Barbara was at that point. She had reached the pinnacle of hatred and rage. They would pay. *That disgusting pig, Mr. Willis, the filthy bastard boy, and his whore of a mother!*

Barbara looked out of her bedroom window. Off to the right, through the darkness, she could make out the small balcony outside the window that her mother had climbed out of to get to the roof. For the briefest of moments, Barbara considered repeating her mother's performance.

The sight, the smells, the sounds were etched in her mind, and were still vivid decades later. Wearing a pink dress with white lace, white patent leather Mary Janes, carrying a doll in one hand, and a white purse with a pink poodle, in the other, Barbara remembered skipping up the gravel driveway toward the mansion. She had been at the bank that morning with her father and grandfather. Everyone there was always so nice, but even back then, she knew they had to be. Her daddy was the boss, and her grandpa was an even bigger boss. She loved how special it made her feel. The tellers and managers were all reminded, by her grandfather that Barbara's fifth birthday was coming up, so they gave her coins and candy, which she stuffed into her purse. She did not think to say thank you. She was used to privilege, and she expected it.

Back at home, before little Barbara reached the front door of the mansion, she caught a glimpse of her mother out of the corner of her eye. Ilse Shatsworth was standing, balancing in bare feet, on the highest, steepest pitch of the slate roof. She was wearing a black silk dressing gown, and despite having to keep her balance on the sharp roof peak, she managed to keep an elegant bend to her wrist as she held an opera length, mother of pearl cigarette holder. Barbara could still remember the smell of cigarette smoke combined with the aroma of the freshly cut grass.

"Look at Mother." She smiled at the men, and pointed. The look of shock on her father and grandfather's faces when they looked up, confused Barbara for a moment. She turned back toward her mother just in time to see her land, head first, on the retainer bricks, in front of the short row of hedges.

Over the years, Barbara fed her anger by remembering the crack and thud of her mother hitting the ground. She was not horrified by the sight and sound like the men were. No, not at all. They gasped and recoiled, shocked and sickened. Barbara remembered staring at first, confused and surprised. Then, her lips slowly turned upward at the corners. Her father ran to her and knelt down in front of her. His brows scrunched in confusion when he saw the look on her face. She stood, staring at the bloody and contorted body of her mother, smiling as if she were watching clowns preforming in a circus act. "Mrs. Appleton!" He shouted at the door for the nanny. "Come get my daughter and call the doctor! I think little Barbara is in shock!"

It was a smile born of selfishness, not shock. She was smiling at the time, thinking, *Mother is mean to Daddy, and now she can't be mean to him anymore, and he will spend more time with me!* Now she seethed with disgust for ever having counted on a man for anything. Her father did not spend more time with her after her mother's death. He spent less time with her, and more time with promiscuous women.

Barbara slapped herself to break her obsession with the memories of that day. Her hatred of men had reached a fever pitch. The angrier she became, the better she felt, so she allowed it to consume her. She pictured, in her mind, a boiling sea of flames, filled with evil men – men that she had sent there. *They won't be led around by their dicks anymore when they're burning in hell!* She told herself. *Time to get to it.*

# OMINOUS WHISPERS

## CHAPTER 17

*"She's coming for you, Tom. Your mother's coming!"*
Tom could feel the whispering breath of the house tickling his ear as it warned him. "Ticka, ticka, ticka. It's okay. I won't let her hurt me. I'll run...I'll run away!" Tom whispered. His thigh muscles began to quiver, and the hair stood up on his arms. *No, no, no!* He thought as he tried to run from his bedroom, only to find that his leg muscles were captives of his numbing fear. Tom clenched his fists so tightly that his fingernails dug into his palms, making them bleed. He shook, not only with fear, but with hatred. He hated himself, he hated being her victim, he hated his gutless father, but most of all he hated her.

# TAMMY GACH

Stinging, burning, aching – oh yes, without a doubt – she would dole out plenty of that, but it was the humiliation that she had planned for him, that fed her soul, and filled her with a sense of omnipotence. Barbara clopped from room to room, gathering items to use as her tools of torture, as casually as a shopper picking out items at a grocery store. *I've never thought to use this before!* She snorted with sadistic anticipation, as she took Mr. Willis's leather razor strap from the bathroom near his den. As she plodded down the hall, past the foyer, something perfect caught her eye. She kept a bowling pin next to the main entry, to ward off intruders, should she ever encounter any at her front door. *How fortuitous!* Surges of adrenaline gushed through Barbara's body, making her skin tingle, as her diseased mind pictured the grotesque things that she could do to Tom with the bowling pin. In a near manic fervor, she practically ran down the huge foyer to get the bowling pin. (Pigs have been known to run a seven minute mile, but Barbara Willis was nowhere close to breaking that record!).

One of her demented thoughts, in particular, excited her more than the others, but it also caused her to imagine the vile things that her Mr. Willis and the woman in the photos did when they were together. *His whore probably lets him stick it into any hole he wants! Men are nothing more than depraved, sex crazed perverts! I think it's about time that*

110

# OMINOUS WHISPERS

*they find out what it feels like to be one of their whores,*
*and why ladies don't allow that sort of deviant behavior.*

A cold, black fog trailed behind Barbara as she made her way to the grand staircase that led to the second floor bedrooms. The foggy mist that sucked the heat from Barbara's body was colder and blacker than usual. It poured from her. Most of it seeped into the walls of the hallway, but it was so thick that some of it lingered, swirling through the air like a cloud of gnats. Barbara was grateful for the sucking of heat from her body. She was perpetually sweaty, and, often times, Tom had to apply medication and talc to the skin folds that she could not reach.

Her enjoyment of the cold began to diminish, the closer she got to Tom's room. With each step, the Persian rug felt stickier and stickier, holding her feet, as if she were an insect trying to walk across fly paper. The more she fought to take a step, the thicker the black fog became. As the walls became saturated with the evil that emanated from her, her steps became lighter, and the Persian rug no longer felt like fly paper.

When Barbara reached the closed door of Tom's bedroom, she set her sundry of torture tools out of sight, on the floor against the wall. Barbara had no intention of knocking today. She simply turned the doorknob. She was

111

surprised and angered to find the door locked. He had never locked it before. He was warned about that. *That willful little shit!* She seethed. *He disobeyed me on purpose! After this, he won't make that mistake again!*

"Mr. Willis! You unlock this door right now!" She insisted.

"I won't!" His voice, wet and muffled, crackled with fear.

Clenching her jaw, fierce with anger, she heard the sound of a tooth cracking in her mouth. She wanted to take an ax, and break the door down, but that would take too much work. Her brain squirmed, considering ways to get in. She was not going to be denied even if she had to burn her mansion down to get to him. "Okay, Thomas." She lied. "Mother has had a couple of very difficult days, and I am tired. I took some time to examine how dreadfully I have been treating you and your father, and I desperately want to change...I need to change...for you." She paused, and heard nothing, so she added, "May I come in for a few minutes so we can just talk?"

Barbara had never been that nice to him, before, or to anyone for that matter. Tom was hesitant, but like a neophyte, he fell for her deceit.

## OMINOUS WHISPERS

It was heavier than she had expected. Her arms quivered with strain, but she managed to keep her newly discovered instrument of torture, hidden behind her back.

"Sit down, Thomas. I'm tired, and I simply want to talk." Barbara reiterated. The feigned look of innocence seemed genuine to Tom, but he could hear the whispers pleading with him – *no, no, no!* Even without the soft whisper of admonition, Tom knew better than to sit on his bed. Too many bad things had happened to him there. He turned around to get the chair from his desk behind him. Chair in hand, he turned and looked up just in time to see the bowling pin that his mother kept near the front door for intruders, coming straight at his forehead.

Tom slowly regained consciousness. It took him a moment to remember how he came to be sprawled, face down, on his bedroom floor, and a couple more moments to realize what that strange sensation was, that had brought him back to consciousness. At first, the warmth that was spilling across the side of his head and face confused him. *I'm not in the bathtub.* He thought. *I'm in my bedroom.* He began to put his hands toward his face to wipe the water from it, but he could not. The shock that spread through him, made his heart pound harder and faster. With each beat, the intensity of the pain from the knot on his forehead, increased - like blows from a hammer driving a nail deeper and deeper into a piece of wood. The head-pounding shock came when he realized that he was naked, with his hands and feet tied behind his back, connected to a rope around his neck. Every movement of his limbs pulled on the rope around his neck, causing him to gag and become light-headed. Tom's eyes started feeling as if the inside of his eyelids were made of sandpaper. He could see the fat, white mounds of skin that poured over his mother's black, square heeled pump, as she stood next to him. Suddenly, it dawned on him that it wasn't bath water streaming down his face. His mother was standing, straddled over his head, urinating on him.

"Untie me! Untie me! I'll be good, I promise!" Tom cried and choked as the rope around his neck tightened with every plea. He closed his eyes tightly, hoping that the burning pain from his mother's piss would subside.

With his eyes still closed, Tom could feel the enormity of her presence as she stepped away from his head. Terror filled every part of him. His stomach rolled and churned as if he had swallowed a squirming snake. He thought that he would vomit at any moment, but he really did not care. His entire body shivered, because he knew that she was not done. He tried to imagine how he would kill her, if he got out of this alive, but his mind was too paralyzed with the fear of what she would do next.

# OMINOUS WHISPERS

"That's right, you filthy coward! Close your eyes! Do your tramps and prostitutes close their eyes while you violate them?" She hissed with disdain. The pair of scissors that Barbara had used to cut Tom's clothes off, was too close to his tied hands, for her comfort, so she kicked them further away. Her son was a freakishly huge man, and she was not certain that the ropes would hold. His squirming stomach gave way, and vomit shot from his mouth when he felt her trying to spread his butt cheeks. He clenched down as tight as he could, but her hate filled rage gave her strength. He clamped his butt muscles with a fervor, refusing to be entered.

Tom felt a brief moment of victory when she took her hands off of his backside. His victory was short-lived. He felt something cold and hard being pushed against him. He clenched tight again. It was not her hands this time. He did not have time to figure out what the object was, before he heard a crack, like steel smashing into wood. Tom howled and jerked his body with such force, at the sudden, ripping pain, that it was a wonder the rope did not snap his neck. A fierce whack on the bottom of the bowling pin from Barbara's hammer, drove the top part of it into him, tearing his flesh along the way. Tom felt the stabbing agony shoot all the way up to his shoulder blades, so he assumed that she had impaled him clean through.

# TAMMY GACH

Blackness crept inward, narrowing Tom's field of vision. He used the fear and rage that he felt, to keep from passing out. Icy chills and burning waves of heat, mingled in a painful dance throughout his body. He could make out the vulgar image of his mother bending down near the door to his room. He allowed his eyes to close for a moment as he hoped and prayed that she was leaving him alone so he could die in peace. The sound of his desk chair creaking and cracking under the strain of Barbara's weight, made Tom open his eyes. Despair took hold of him when he saw that she was still there. She gave a sigh of exhaustion, wiped the sweat from her brow, and then put a full fifth of scotch to her lips. She tipped her head back and continued to gulp loudly until half the bottle was empty.

Barbara remained plopped on the chair, a bloated, hunched, lump of inhumanity, staring at Tom until the booze kicked-in. Sufficiently soused, Barbara stood and stumbled toward Tom. He began to cry as he pleaded with her, "Please don't hurt me anymore!"

"Oh, shut up! You act like I'm going to kill you!" She said in a drunken slur, the half empty bottle of booze still tightly clenched in her fist. She took another swig, bent down, and nearly fell over as she removed the bowling pin from his torn rectum. She tossed it on the floor in front of

Tom's face. His despair quickly turned to disbelief, then to rage when he saw the bowling pin painted in his blood.

*She's gonna pay for this!* He promised himself.

Tom was just about to use his rage to get free from the ropes, or to die trying, when Barbara started to untie him. The spinning in her head got worse every time she bent over, so she tried to lower herself to her knees. Snorts and grunts came from her booze soaked breath as she struggled to keep her balance. Almost...almost, then...thud! She lost what little balance she had, and crashed down, half on Tom, and half on the floor. She was saying something in a drunken babble as she sat up and continued to untie the ropes, but Tom was not listening. He was plotting revenge.

Finally untied, Tom got to his feet. His first reaction was to grab that bowling pin and smash her skull in with it, but as soon as he bent over to get it, blood started running down his legs. Mortified, and afraid he was bleeding to death, he ran out of the room and locked himself in the bathroom. He sat on the toilet and sobbed as the pain continued to rip through him. Tom looked toward the bathroom door. His heart gave him a single, hard kick, and with a sudden gasp, he ducked his head, covering it with his arms. His mother's eyes were glaring at him with a blood red hatred, as she took another swing

117

at his head with the blood stained bowling pin. With his head low, safely tucked beneath his arms, Tom sat, eyes closed, trembling, and waiting. After a moment, he realized that he did not get hit, and he did not hear anything either – he did not hear the clopping of her shoes, like a massive hoofed beast, on the tile floor, and he did not hear any of the grunts or snorts commonly produced by the exertions of his grossly obese mother. He parted his arms, and cautiously looked around the room. She was not there, and it scared him when he realized that she had not been in the bathroom. Tom gently ran his fingers across his forehead. The knot was huge, and painful to the slightest touch. *No wonder I'm seeing things!* He thought. *The lying witch nearly caved my skull in!*

Tom also realized, as he sat on the toilet, the bleeding from his rectum and colon must have stopped because he could no longer feel it streaming from him, or hear the splashing as it hit the toilet water. He was right, the bleeding had stopped, but he was not prepared for the horror that gripped him when he looked and saw that the toilet water was bright red, and golf ball sized blood clots lined the sides of the bowl. Tom dropped to his knees as a tidal wave of dizzying nausea hit, causing his stomach to spasm with dry heaves. There was nothing left in his stomach to come out, but the force alone was enough to start the rectal bleeding again.

# OMINOUS WHISPERS

The pain and the blood, and the nausea, and the humiliation were the grotesque gifts given to him by a psychotic mother, and purchased by a weak and selfish father who was afraid of her. *Ticka, ticka, ticka* ran through his head on repeat, as he sat on the bathroom floor, bleeding. *"It's time to take control, Tom."* The whispers comforted him. He could feel the strength welling up inside of him, lifting him like hot air fills and lifts a balloon. *"Far too much evil has seeped in. It's eating my very spirit and soul."* The whispers of the mansion on Knob Hill, softly cried to Tom. *"The same way that termites infest and eat houses – bit by bit."*

Tom knew that the whispers were right. Anger and mental anguish kept building. His mind jumped and swirled from one evil image to another. Image after image popped up from their hiding places, deep in the darkest corners of his mind, like the mole in the arcade game, trying to avoid the hammer.

The images and memories were taunting him – the way that the children taunted him before his parents pulled him out of school. The grotesque images were evil snapshots, pushing and pushing him to take action – to make the taunting stop. Flash! Flash! The brown skin tags that lined the pasty white folds of his mother's neck, getting closer and closer. The look of elation on his mother's face as he was forced to endure the searing pain of the scalding

119

bath. Flash! Flash! The fondling and scrubbing of his penis and scrotum until they were raw and bleeding, and the germs were dead. The look of disgust on Alfred's face when Tom was six years old, and his father told his mother to "Keep the little retard out of public, because he'll ruin my reputation and tarnish the family name." Flash! Flash! His mother's burning, stinking urine running in his eyes, nose and mouth. The orange and white guinea pig as it went limp in the squeezing hands of a huge six year old. Tears of anger and frustration welled up in Tom's eyes when the image of the guinea pig flashed through his mind. He wiped the tears from his eyes and the drips from his nose as he thought, *I never meant to hurt that poor little animal. They were all teasing me, and a couple of the boys were throwing toys at me! IT JUST HAPPENED AND I NEVER MEANT IT!*

The painful images stopped taunting him. At least for now. An eerie calm, unlike anything he had ever felt before – except when the whispers came – enveloped Tom. A fierce determination to take control of his own life was building, as was his plan to rip that control away from his parents. He grabbed a towel, wiped the blood from his torn anus and from the floor, then he grabbed another towel to cover his front, before heading back to his bedroom to put some clothes on, and to bludgeon his mother to death.

120

## OMINOUS WHISPERS

Barbara was still on the floor, drunkenly babbling to herself when Tom walked in. He went to his closet and put on a tee shirt and a soft pair of sweat pants. His eyes were glazed over with a vacant stare, kind of like the whole fish that you see packed in ice at the grocery store. Every bit of his fear was gone. The fear, anxiety, self-doubt and self-loathing that his parents nurtured in him, and that had plagued him his entire life, simply was not there. She had gone too far this time. He had long since grown numb to the shame and nausea that he felt every time she forced him to sexually satisfy her. He had been having to do that since he was a child, but the sodomy - she had never done *that* before.

He stood, towering over his mother, with his dead fish eyes staring, as she managed to pull her drunken heft from the floor onto his bed. He looked at the bowling pin, the hammer, and the scissors that were still on the floor. *Look at her just lying there.* He thought. *Too drunk and too tired to even fight back. A couple of whacks on the head, and done!* Tom put his hand to his chin, and scrunched his eyebrows. He paused as the thought came to him. *That would be too quick. She has tortured and abused me for as long as I can remember, and today, she damaged and humiliated me. No. She doesn't deserve quick.*

## CHAPTER 18

Every step of the way to the maintenance shed, shot a throbbing arrow of pain from Tom's rectum, up the sides of his abdomen. Images of that damned bowling pin kept flashing through his tormented, yet strangely calm mind. He was no longer brimming over with anger and humiliation. Just physical pain, and an overwhelming need to carry out his plan. The plan that was forming, clearer by the minute, that would show both of his parents that he's the boss now, and no one would ever humiliate him again.

In the distance, he could hear the faint whispers of the mansion. *"Don't become like them, Tom. Don't dump any more evil here. It's up to you. It's always been up to you. There has never been a more innocent soul to walk these halls than you, Tom. That's why only you can feel and hear the gentle essence – the heart – the soul of Knob Hill.*

122

# OMINOUS WHISPERS

Without emotion, Tom turned his cold gaze back to the task at hand. This was the first time that Tom tuned out the benevolent whispers of Knob Hill. He had to. At least until it was over.

"Perfect!" Tom said, when he flipped the light switch in the shed, and noticed the roll of chain near the door. He pulled the bolt cutter down from its outlined space on the peg board of tools, and wondered why he had not spent more time in the maintenance shed when he was growing up. It was huge, and had just about every cool tool and supply needed to maintain or repair any part of the mansion or grounds of Knob Hill. *Mother never goes outside.* He thought. *Maybe if I would have spent time out here building things, instead of sitting in my room watching TV, she wouldn't have had as many opportunities to scald me in the tub, or...Stop it! Just stop!* He thought, promising himself that he would never go through anything like that, ever again.

Tom cut two lengths of chain, each about ten feet long. He gathered some wood screws, washers, and a couple of, still new in the package, padlocks with keys, and took them inside, to the basement. He screwed one end of each chain, into an overhead wooden beam, using washers to keep the chain from pulling away from the screws. He took the padlocks out of the packages, and hooked one through the end link of each chain, without locking them. The corner of Tom's lip curled up in satisfaction as he looked at the locks. *She thinks I'm stupid? Well, maybe she'll think again when she finds herself chained up!* He scoffed.

Tom limped, still in fierce pain, over to a mattress that was leaning against the wall. He grabbed it to pull it over to the chains, then he stopped for a moment. *I should just make her fat ass sit on the cold, damp cement floor! She doesn't deserve a mattress!*

He sneezed when the mildew and dust wafted from the stained, filthy mattress, and hit his nose. Tom dropped the mattress and doubled over. Pain shot, like a blow torch, through his sides and rectum, when he sneezed. He breathed through his mouth, in short, shallow huffs, until the pain subsided. He put the collar of his tee shirt over his nose and mouth, and dragged the stinking mattress to the chains, knowing that his mother hated the smell of mildew, more than she would hate sitting on a cold floor.

The loathing of his parents was the driving force that Tom used to help him make it up the basement stairs, and then to his father's study, at the opposite end of the nineteen room mansion. He took a double barrel, break-action, side by side shotgun from the display case that had once belonged to his great grandfather. He grabbed two shotgun shells from the box that was sitting next to the gun, and then he made his way back to the maintenance shed.

## OMINOUS WHISPERS

He remembered reading, in one of the Westerns that he had loved in his early teen years, about a cattle thief who sawed off the end of his shotgun after his brothers joked that he could not hit the broad side of a barn. Tom had no idea how well he could shoot, but he did know that his mother always called him a clumsy oaf, so a wider spray might just come in handy tomorrow.

Tom set the gun on the work bench, and took a hack saw from the peg board. He held the gun down with the barrels off the end of the bench, and sawed them off almost to the wood at the fore end. He was surprised that the metal was soft enough to be cut without difficulty. Tom had never thought much about guns before, just like he had never thought much about the maintenance shed before, either. The gun felt nice, and he understood why his great grandfather liked to collect and shoot guns as a hobby. The coolness of the metal contrasted with the smooth warmth of the wood. He became lost in the moment, caressing and exploring its intricacies, until a sudden sharp pain pierced his index finger. Jarred from his tactile trance, Tom looked at the curved sliver of gunmetal sticking from his finger. Concerned more for the gun than for his finger, he plucked the long shard from his finger, and then furrowed his eyebrows as he examined the sawed barrel with meticulous concern. He took a fine tooth file from the peg board, and gently filed the rough end until it was as smooth as the beautifully ornate scrolls of mahogany in the piano room.

Tom felt a rush of self-pride as he slid the two 12 gauge shells into their side by side chambers. *God, I should have done this sooner!* He thought, as he basked in the glorious feeling of control that he had never before experienced.

The corner of Tom's upper lip quivered in a spontaneous sneer as he recalled his father's booming voice during a phone conversation a year or two earlier. *Maybe if you were a bit more proactive, and a bit less reactive when it comes to dealing with your mother, you wouldn't have to bother me at work! You know better than to call here!*

Tom had been trying to tell his father about the physical abuse and molestation by his mother, for several years. He never realized that his father already knew that he was being used as his sexual proxy, and that it was simply easier to ignore it, than to get into the messy middle of it. It became nauseatingly clear earlier today, as he sat sodomized and bleeding on the bathroom floor. *You want proactive, Dad? Well, I can do that! Will you be proud of me, or will you choke to death on those words, and your own hypocrisy! Guess we'll have to wait and see.*

## OMINOUS WHISPERS

## CHAPTER 19

Like a baby bird poking its way out of an egg shell, bit by bit, minute by minute, Tom's confidence grew coldly strong, and the physical pain of his abuse, diminished in tandem. He picked up a pair of work gloves that someone had left on the bench, and then, with less of a limp, and with more of a purpose, he walked back up to the house, shotgun in hand. He went to the hall coat closet and found his knit ski cap, and the camo jacket that his mother absolutely hated. The jacket had been given to him by Ernie, the same kindly maintenance man who taught Tom to drive and how to fix a flat tire.

Tom went up the main staircase, stepping over the creaking stair out of habit this time, rather than trepidation that his mother might hear him. He did not care if she heard or saw him, so he did not try to be at all quiet when he opened his bedroom door and walked in. Still sprawled out drunk and half oozing off the side of his bed, Barbara heard him come in the room. She barked a command without raising her head. "Be useful for once, and get me a bucket! I need to puke!"

Tom felt his fists tighten around the gun. He raised it and aimed it at her head. "Pow!" He said as he pretended to pull the trigger. He ached with the desire to just shoot her, and to be done with it. But what he really wanted was for her to wake up and be able to walk, because he had no intention of carrying over three hundred pounds of dead weight down to the shackles that were waiting for her in the basement. He poked the motionless, globular woman with the shortened barrel of the gun, but it was clear to him that his mother would not be standing up any time soon. He decided to set about getting the clothes, boots and duffel bag from his closet that he would need in the morning. He would get to her later.

After he collected his supplies, he walked over to his mother and stood, staring at her for a moment. His eyes, still cold and dead, were a reflection of the emptiness of his soul. The cold, dark fog still circled around Barbara, enveloping her in its icy clutches of evil hatred. Tom grabbed the wastepaper basket next to his desk, and slammed it down on the floor beneath her head. The bitter stinging cold of the black fog, grabbed and clawed at his huge arm as he reached through it to deliver the puke bucket. Startled, he quickly pulled his arm from the piercing cold fog, to find jagged, bloody scratches running the length of his forearm.

*Ticka, ticka, ticka...No! Stop it!* Tom scolded himself as he backed out of the bedroom. He did not want to fall back into fear and insecurity. He would not allow himself to lose the vindictive anger that was fueling him. He knew that he would need it.

*"Tom, the evil is trying to destroy you! Can't you see, Tom? Can't you see that you can't let that happen? Don't become like them! If you do this, you will have become just like your parents!"* The whispers of the mansion became louder with each plea.

Tom covered his ears and squeezed his eyes shut. "No! *You* can't see!" Tom shouted at the walls of the mansion. "I have to do this! They have to be taught a lesson that they won't forget! They have to see that I won't let them hurt me ANYMORE!"

*"You know that you're smart, and you know that you're strong! But, what you don't know is that they are weak and selfish, and they can't feel good about themselves*

129

*without hurting or using someone else. I have seen generations of them claw and scratch their way to the top up the backs of good people like you and Jeff ... "*

In a wide eyed frenzy, Tom whipped his head around, looking for the whispers, that he knew, he could not see.

"What do you know about Jeff? How can a house know?"

*I know everything here, and I know the hearts, minds and souls of everyone who comes here. They all leave traces of themselves behind, in the very foundation of this structure. Their deeds saturate the essence of Knob Hill like colorful dye saturates the shell of an Easter egg. They make me what I am. So, if you do this, if you do evil things, you will add to the decay of this beautiful mansion.*

The longer the whispers spoke to him, the less melodious they sounded. Tom took his supplies for the next morning, some snacks, and couple of bottles of root beer, and left the house. "Na-na-na-na-na." Tom shouted to drown out the whispers that were becoming as irritating as nails on a chalk board.

Tom hopped into the drab, green van that was there for the use of the estate's caretakers. He pulled up the driver's side floor mat, and found the keys, right where the workers always left them. He reclined the seat, put his hands over his ears, and rocked back and forth as he repeated *ticka, ticka, ticka,* until he drowned out the shrill whispers, and drifted off to sleep.

TAMMY GACH

CHAPTER 20

AUGUST 24, 1978

The chirping of the birds in the tree that canopied the van, woke Tom. The sun was up, and it was already a stifling hot day. He raised the back of the seat, and rolled down the only two windows that the van had, hoping to feel a draft that did not exist. When he stepped out of the van to take a leak on the grass, he found that it was much hotter inside the van than it was outside. He could not let that bother him. He got back into the driver's seat, ate the entire box of glazed chocolate doughnuts, and washed them down with both bottles of root beer. As much as he dreaded it, on such a hot day, he knew that he did not have a choice – he could not chance being recognized, so he climbed into the back of the rusty old van, and put on the long pants, the camo jacket, boots, work gloves, and most uncomfortable of all, the knitted ski mask.

Pouring with sticky sweat beneath his heavy clothing, the only breeze he could feel coming in from the open windows, was on his exposed eye lids and lips. The closer he got to his destination, the more irritated he became from the suffocating heat that was cooking him beneath his clothes, and the maddening itch of his scalp beneath the sweat soaked ski mask.

Livid with rage from the heat, from the pain of his torn rectum, and from every bit of ridicule and indignity that he had suffered throughout his nineteen year existence, Tom parked the van at the curb just outside the door, grabbed his gun and duffel bag, stepped out, and entered his father's bank.

PART II

CHAPTER 21

August 24, 1978

"Stay down and stay quiet or I'll shoot you!" Tom shouted at Sandy as he hurled her into the back of his van. The force of his push sent her skidding head first across the rust coated floor of the cargo bed. Her long hair became caught between her hands and the floor, ripping out two big chunks. She looked at the strands of long hair and orange rust that were stuck to her scraped, sweating palms, but she could not register any pain. She wanted desperately to scream and fight and claw at the van door as it slammed shut, but she was still paralyzed by fear. As the van sped away, Sandy's instinct to survive kicked in. *Where is he taking me and why*? She wondered. The *why* terrified her more than the *where*. She wanted to cry so badly, but she knew that she had to start thinking if she wanted to live. As her shock gave way to rational thought, the pain of the pent up tears and anguish set in, aching like a kick to the throat.

Sandy looked around the best she could without moving too much. She could see his angry red eyes glare at her every few seconds in the rear view mirror which he had aimed at her. He had removed his ski mask, but his head was so huge that the only feature of his that she could see in the mirror, were those angry, beady bloodshot eyes. There were no windows in the back of the van, but she knew that she needed to see landmarks if she wanted to know where they were going. She tried to catch glimpses through the windshield, without him noticing.

Sandy remembered that she had looked at the clock earlier when she saw Ted in the bank. It seemed to her as if hours had passed since then, but a quick glance at her watch told her that only ten minutes had gone by.

The pain in Sandy's throat from fighting back tears was beginning to be replaced with a need to vomit. The stench of mildew and putrid body odor rolled off the huge man's sweat soaked clothing like a putrid wave. The extreme heat and humidity that was trapped inside the rusty old van, intensified the fetid air that enveloped her.

Another five minutes had passed. Sandy was certain that she would be dead soon from heat exhaustion, so she began to silently pray. *God, please forgive me for all my sins. And Mom, I might be coming to join you, so please be waiting for me when I get to heaven....* As she was praying, she felt the van slow down and turn onto what sounded like a gravel road. After a moment she could hear tall grass or weeds brushing along the bottom of the van. The van came to a stop, and the driver glared at Sandy one last time, in the rear view mirror, before he got out. She could hear his heavy footsteps as he shuffled through dry grass to the back of the van. When he opened the back doors, her eyes burned and filled with tears, as she struggled to adjust to the bright sunlight that silhouetted the stinking, hulking figure from behind.

"Get out of the van and don't try to run." He commanded. As her eyes adjusted, she could see that he had removed all of his clothing except his filthy brown corduroy pants and his boots. It was her first real look at him, and she wanted to memorize every detail about him and about their location. She was determined to escape, and she wanted to give the police enough information to find him and throw his ass in jail.

136

# OMINOUS WHISPERS

He was younger than she thought; maybe early twenties at most. His dark hair was saturated with sweat, grease and dandruff. His skin was pasty white and devoid of body hair, as if it belonged to a bloated carcass that had washed up on a beach. Pinkish stretch marks, which looked like scratches from a deranged tiger, lined his obese abdomen. His overly large red nipples were puffy and made him look as if he could be a wet nurse.

Sandy looked around as he pulled her by the arm toward a house – a huge house. She could not see a road other than the long gravel driveway, through which they had entered the property. Beyond that, and in every direction, all she could see was trees. He still had the sawed off shotgun with him, but she knew that she had to try to get away while she was still outside. With sudden and decisive force, she pulled her arm from his sweaty grasp and ran as fast as she could back toward the gravel driveway.

"Shit!" he shouted as he started to run after her. She did not look back, but she could hear that his heavy grunting and footsteps were becoming further and further in the distance as she hit the gravel of the driveway in a full out sprint.

A pain that felt like fire sprayed the back of her right calf and ankle at the same instant that she heard the

thunderous crack of the shotgun.  She was still running.
*Maybe he didn't hit me directly!  Maybe he hit the gravel,
and that's what sprayed my leg!* She hoped.  Her hope was
brief.  Both legs started to feel heavy and her right shoe
started to feel wet.  Her stride slowed.  The last thing she
remembered was the stinking, sweaty flesh of her abductor
as he tackled her, and drove her down hard into the gravel.

OMINOUS WHISPERS

CHAPTER 22

Sandy came to in a blurry haze of pain and confusion. As her vision became less blurred, her pain became more intense. It all came back to her when she realized that she was slung over the fat, bare shoulder of her abductor like a sack of potatoes. Her first thought was to hit and kick and scramble like a wild, trapped animal, but her body was torn and broken and refused to respond to her commands to fight.

She could only see down and a bit from side to side. Sandy saw that he was carrying her across a black and white checkerboard floor that was huge and looked like marble. It did not make sense. A shack in the woods would have been more in character with his outward appearance. *Does he live here?* Sandy began to wonder how they would ever find her, if she, herself, couldn't tell where she was. *Is this a mansion, or a museum, or a funeral home?* Sandy wondered. It did not add up. This man, who had her slung over his shoulder, with her face right in front of his exposed, lint encrusted butt crack, was anything but refined. Not at all the kind of person that she would have imagined to live in such a grand place.

The thunderstorm of pain raging in Sandy's head was starting to subside. Still slung over his shoulder, she did her best to notice every detail. Her abductor turned right at the end of the grand foyer, and started down a wide wood paneled hallway. The second doorway on the left led into a huge kitchen. The cold sterility of the stainless steel, and white tiles made Sandy realize that it was not a family style kitchen; it was more like an industrial or restaurant type kitchen. He went in and walked past a center island and a commercial range. *Shit! Move to the left fat ass! Move to the left, just two feet!* Sandy screamed at him in her mind. Had he done so, she could have reached one of the three chef's knives that were on the center island.

Just past the range, he leaned forward and she tumbled off his sweaty shoulder. Sandy bit back her pain when she hit the ground. A sound, more like a whimper came from her, rather than the wail that she wanted to cry. He still had that damned shotgun. Regardless, she knew that she could not run, not even if her life depended on it – which it did. She could not feel her right leg at all from the knee down. It was still there, her dress slacks blasted into the exposed muscle of her calf. It looked as if someone had taken shreds of cloth, and put them into a meat grinder along with a chunk of bloody, red beef. She began to vomit and almost blacked out when she saw it, but the pain, from her broken ribs, snapped her back to awareness.

Directly in front of where Sandy lay, crumpled on the kitchen floor, was a stretch of wood paneled wall that was painted white like the rest of the kitchen. Her abductor pushed on it, and it sprang back a bit toward him. *Oh, God no,* was her first thought when she saw that it was a concealed door. Another wave of terror washed over her as she wondered what horrible things were awaiting her on the other side.

"Come on. We're going to go down here." He used his sawed off shotgun to point to the stairway on the other side of the secret door.

"No, please Mr. I...I don't want to go anywhere but home." Her eyes were as big as saucers. Her voice quivered and her words wavered like a bad recording.

141

C..can't you s..see that I'm hurt and b..b..bleeding?" Sandy pleaded with her abductor, trying to make some kind, any kind of human connection with him.

He looked at her leg, and cocked his head, as if he were realizing for the first time that she was injured. "Ticka, ticka, ticka." He nervously shifted his huge frame from foot to foot, chewed off a piece of his fingernail and spit it out on the floor. "I shouldn't have done that. Ticka, ticka. But you shouldn't have run when I very clearly told you not to!"

"Are you going to kill me?" Sandy asked, immediately regretting asking the question that she did not want to hear the answer to. *Of course he's going to kill you, you idiot! First he's going to rape you, then he's going to kill you. Stupid question!* Sandy scolded herself silently.

"NO I'M NOT GOING TO KILL YOU!" His eyebrows furled and his huge round face became red. He was riding on the edge of his raw emotions, like a cat walking atop a shaky fence, so he could not tell if he was more hurt or angered by her question. "Can you make it down those stairs, or do I have to carry you?"

Cringing at the thought of him touching her again, Sandy decided that if she *had* to go down those stairs, that she would rather die falling down them than to have him

142

touch her. "I'LL MANAGE!" she surprised herself that she snapped at him. A moment earlier, she was having trouble getting her words out, but now, like a switch in her head got flipped, she was PISSED! Her pain and lack of control over her situation was making her angry. Angrier than she had ever been.

Pain and anger. Captor and captive had that in common.

# CHAPTER 23

The stairs behind the secret doorway led down to a musty smelling, damp basement. The floor and walls were cement that was cracked in places from the shifting and settling of the huge old mansion over the years. Two long chains hung down from a wooden rafter beam above a very old, stained mattress that was laying on the damp concrete. On the end of each chain was a padlock. The top end of the chains were secured to the beam with what looked to Sandy like a screw through a washer that was wider than the link of chain. "Oh no! – Hell no! – Nnn...no! Sandy cried, panicked by the thought of being chained. *Keep*

OMINOUS WHISPERS

*your head, keep your head! If you want to stay alive you're going to have to think your way out of this!* She told herself. *That wood rafter is old. You WILL be able to rip those screws out if you work at it.*

Sandy's eyes darted around, and her head turned in every direction, like a cat trying to catch a laser light. She could see that the part of the basement that they were in was partitioned off from God knows what else there was in the rest of the basement. In this part, there was a lot of dusty, cobweb covered junk. Old picture frames, wicker baskets, bundles of newspapers and magazines, but most important of all, there was a hinged window, large enough to crawl through, about five feet above the floor on the far wall.

It was still light outside, and she could see that there were no bars on the window, and it was in direct view of where he was about to chain her. *Ignore the pain! Don't you fucking cry and God damn it don't you pass out!* In her mind, Sandy was declaring this war, and she was being her own drill sergeant.

"Go over there and sit on that mattress." Her abductor said.

Sandy had scooted down the basement stairs on her butt. She had tried hopping, but, with each hop, pain

145

seared through her broken ribs like a blow torch. She started to scoot the twenty feet or so toward the mattress. "Wait. Here, let me help you." The huge man said, then gently lifted her up as if she were as light as a feather. Sandy saw a slight glimmer of humanity in those beady porcine-like eyes of his that took her by surprise.

*He's empathizing!* She was confused, but then she also remembered the look on his face when she had asked him if he was going to kill her. *Talk to him San, talk to him. Try to get through to him! Talk to him - talk your way out of this!* She told herself.

"I'm going to put these chains around your wrists and lock them." He said as he put her down on the mattress.

"Why?" She asked.

He gave a slight chuckle of amusement. "What do you mean, why? So you don't run away."

"Do I look like I can run?" Sandy said, trying to play on his amusement, but it nearly backfired.

"I didn't mean to hurt you! I DIDN'T, I DIDN'T, I DIDN'T!" He stomped his feet like an angry toddler.

"It's OK, calm down." She said in the most soothing tone that she could manage. "Can I ask you why you are doing this? I mean, these chains were already here. Were you planning to take *me* specifically, or have you done this before?" Sandy was surprised that she could talk so calmly. She was *plenty* terrified, but somehow, talking to her huge captor was calming them both.

His eyes narrowed as he looked at her and studied her face for a moment. "Ticka, ticka, ticka, ticka." He said in almost a whisper as he began to pace and rub the sweat from his hands on the front of his corduroy pants. "OK, OK." He said, pointing a warning finger at her. "I'll answer you, but don't call me stupid!"

*Stupid? Why would he say that?* It was clear to her that his psyche got messed up at some point in his life – And if he had an axe to grind, she could only pray that he would not take it out on her, at least not more that he already had. "No. Of course not." Sandy said, shaking her head.

She could hear the loose snot rattle around in his nose as he took an exceptionally huge, deep breath before he started his rant. "These chains weren't for you. I wasn't planning on *taking* anyone. I don't even know who you are. I got pissed off, because, once again, my father wouldn't listen! He just wouldn't listen to me! And I had a fucking gun and he still was telling me what to do! I shoulda shot his useless ass right there in the bank, but that isn't what I went there to do. I went there to teach him – him and my mother - a lesson! Ticka, ticka the one who

147

needs killing is my mother. She's the one the chains are for! NO MORE FUCKING BATHS, AND NO MORE SLEEPING WITH HER BECAUSE MY FUCKING FATHER WON'T DO IT ANYMORE! Ticka, ticka, ticka…" He sat down next to her on the mattress, huddled into a ball and rocked back and forth.

Sandy had never felt so many conflicting emotions at once before. Horror, fear, pity, anger, pain, sympathy. *Is Mr. Willis this guy's father? Is this the half-brother that Jeff was telling me about?* Sandy's head throbbed. She was even more confused now. She remembered years ago, when her mother was alive, Mr. Willis would come to the house for dinner. Mrs. Willis was always too sick to come. They were family friends. That's why Willis gave her a teller job when she was only seventeen. *Now that I think of it, my mom did always ask how their son was – little, somebody? – I don't remember the name, but shit, yeah, I think the Willis' did have a kid!*

*This guy has way more problems than Jeff seems to know about.* Sandy thought. *It may be my ticket out. Maybe if I listen to him, maybe he'll let me go.* It was worth a try, she thought.

"I might be able to help, you know. Or maybe just listen. People tell me I'm a good listener." Sandy worried that she would push him too far, or that maybe he was a complete psycho and really did not care if anybody listened. But she sensed that there was a real human under this monster exterior. A human who had been abused for far too long.

Waves of pain, some dull, and some sharp, washed over Sandy's torso and leg as she sat, in chains, listening to this huge man-child tell his life story of abuse, molestation and madness. *How could my parents, my mom – the mom on the eternal pedestal – have been friends with such monsters? Oh my God! My dad!* Sandy's thoughts shifted back to her present reality. *He's gotta be worried to death about me – I'm worried to death about me! Please, please God, and Mom if you can hear me, please get me out of this alive.*

"I don't even know if my father knows that she makes me fuck her. If he does, I don't think he would even care. That's the problem with him. He's so selfish that it makes me sick." The huge, huddled man wiped the tears and thick ropes of snot from his face with his hand, wiped his hand on the mattress, and then sucked the rest back in through his nose. "The fucker took her side when she pulled me out of school. They said they were worried that I would hurt somebody. I don't know – I mighta – they all picked on me because I was big. I think he doesn't want anyone to see anything about him that isn't perfect. 'My reputation, my reputation!' He whines at her. He *knows* that my mother's crazy, and she *knows* that he married her for her family's money. I don't think that she was always a nut job because he tells her that he wants her to be the way that she used to be. I've only known her as a nut job. Hell, she's more than a nut job – she's a total fucking raving, child molesting lunatic. She takes it out on me, and he's just happy that it's not him. That's why I did it, you know?" Tom paused his long diatribe, to catch his breath.

So much vile information was pelting Sandy in the head that it was dizzying – like a shit blitz to the mind. "You mean you robbed the bank and kidnapped me to teach your parents a lesson?"

"Yep." He said in a slightly slower pace. Well, the robbery, not the kidnapping. I did that because he still wouldn't listen to me. Not even when I had a gun. I couldn't take it anymore. Mother finally found out, after all these years, that my father has a son with his mistress. Not only that, but I met the kid. He's a good guy. He was nice to me. Someone sent her pictures of my father with his mistress and my brother. That's when she got way meaner with me, with sex, than she ever did before. So I just snapped. I wasn't going to put up with any of it any more. That's what the chains were for. She'd already be chained up here if she weren't too fat to carry. She was too shit-faced drunk to stand up yesterday after she hurt me."

"Tom, right?" Sandy softly asked, looking at his tear streaked face, hoping for eye contact. *Look at me. See me as human, as someone who is nice to you, then maybe you'll let me go.* She hoped and prayed.

"How did you know my name? I didn't tell you, did I?"

"No. You didn't. I know Jeff – your brother. We're friends. He told me about you. He told me that he wanted to meet you, and spend more time with you – you know, like brothers should."

"Really?" Tom's lower lip began to quiver, then his entire body convulsed into full blown sobbing. "That must be true." He gasped between sobs. "You can't just be making it up because you know my name, and his name, and he did come to meet me last night!"

"Last night?" Sandy was confused, and then worried. She wondered if Jeff was still there, being held prisoner in some other part of the house. "Where is he now?"

"I don't know. Maybe he went home, but he's going to come back. He promised."

# TAMMY GACH

It was bitter-sweet to know that Jeff was not there. She wished that he was, because there is strength in numbers, but she was happy to know that he was safe and somewhere – anywhere away from this hell-hole.

Sandy winced from pain as she tried to shift her weight. "I gotta get you outta here. You need a doctor." Tom reached toward his pocket for the keys to the padlocks, but then he hesitated. He scrunched his face and hit his forehead with his fists. "I'm gonna go to jail. Bank robbery, and kidnapping. I'm gonna go to jail." He cried.

"Maybe not." Sandy said. "When the police hear what your parents do to you, they'll understand that you just snapped, and that you're not a bad guy!" Sandy was so close to freedom that she could almost taste it. It was getting dark outside. She could barely make out the window at the far side of the basement, now that light wasn't coming in through it. The only light came from a single bulb that was screwed into a socket that hung from the rafter near Sandy's chains. "Your father must have not turned you into the police, because they haven't come to arrest you. And I don't have to turn you in either. Just drop me off anywhere and I'll say I was blindfolded. I'll say that I have no idea who you are, or where you took me." Through the pain and fear, Sandy managed a warm smile that said *trust me*.

## CHAPTER 24

"Well isn't that sweet!" The voice was shrill and cold and came from behind them. Barbara Willis had emerged from her drunken slumber.

Tom turned and sprang to his feet surprisingly fast for someone so obese. Startled, Sandy turned, firing up that blow torch of pain again. Tom grabbed the sawed off shotgun. *How much did she hear?* They both wondered in that brief moment before Barbara spoke again. Tom noticed that his mother was carrying her shoes. He looked at her feet. They were bare, the fat still indented where it normally spilled over the tops of her shoes. *That's why I couldn't hear you coming down the stairs, you sneaky bitch. You always wear your shoes in the house. You think that you're so clever, sneaking around barefoot. I could blast the smirk right off of your disgusting face.* He thought. And, for a fraction of an instant, Sandy thought that she might be rescued.

Barbara dropped her shoes on the floor. Tom and Sandy quietly watched as she wiggled and wedged her feet into them. Mounds of pasty, white flesh rolled over the tops of the black low heeled pumps, making them look tiny – almost like cloven hooves of a farm animal. She waddled toward the mattress. "So, you robbed *my* family's bank and you grabbed a little trophy whore for yourself." She said.

"She's not a whore, Mother!" Tom yelled as he leveled the shotgun at her head.

"How would you know? Tell me, Tom. How would you know? You're just like your father. Your father doesn't know the difference between a whore and a decent woman either. He's probably with his whore right now!"

*Ticka, ticka...* Tom's conversation with Sandy, and the memory of his brother from the day before, had worn smooth the razor sharp edge of his anger. He needed to think this through. He needed to get Sandy to safety.

*They've all been crazy Tom. She comes from a long line of lunatics.* Tom looked up and stretched his non-existent neck as he tried to hear the soothing voice in the distance. *But not you, Tom. Not you. She's never been able to hear me like you do, so I've never been able to help her. Trust me to help you, Tom. Let's put an end to the pain and anger.*

Tom smiled. Sandy watched the look on his face. It was not a smile of joy or amusement. To Sandy, it looked like a smile of relief. She expected to see Barbara Willis' head explode like a watermelon at the hands of her long abused son, at any moment. Barbara knew better. The house – her family mansion – was talking to her son again. Soothing him and making him behave, just like always.

Tom lowered the shotgun and took a deep, snot-slurping breath through his nose. "It's already dark outside, so I don't expect that Dad will be home tonight. This whole thing probably has you stressed, so we'll go to bed and I'll rub your feet." Tom said to his mother.

*What the hell?* Sandy thought. She was certain that Tom was going take the opportunity to kill his mother – his molester – his captor. *Is this good or bad?* Sandy wondered. *It can't be good.*

"You want to be just like your father after all, don't you?" Barbara was talking to Tom, but she was looking straight down her pugged nose at Sandy, who was silently huddled on the mattress.

155

"Of course not Mother!  Why are you saying that?" Tom's slumped shoulders straightened a bit and his moon face started to turn red. *SHUT YOUR HALF-WIT PIE HOLE!!!* He wanted to scream.

"Because you're not getting rid of the whore!" She shrieked. "You think that you can keep a filthy whore, just like your father does?  Well, Mister Willis, let me tell you – YOU CAN'T!  Especially not in MY house!"  Barbara's voice became more shrill and offensive to the ears, the longer and louder she yelled.

"Fine!" Tom said, trying hard not to sound angry.  "I'll get you into bed, then I'll take her and drop her off where she can be found.  No one will see me and I'll come right home."

"Are you an idiot?"  Barbara asked, as she looked at Tom, and shook her head.  "Silly me!  OF COURSE YOU'RE AN IDIOT!"  She shouted at him.  "You have to kill her, and then get rid of the body."  In true psychopathic fashion, Barbara's demeanor turned on a dime.  The look of rage on her face morphed into a soft, sweet smile, as if someone had flipped the tracks on the psycho train in her head.  "A mother is the only woman that you can trust." She said to Tom, in a cloyingly sweet voice that terrified Sandy.  "She said that she won't turn you in, but let me tell you – that will be the first thing that she does! My, my Tom. You really are stupider than you look!"

Sandy began to cry. She buried her face in her shackled hands and wept silently. She stood a chance when it was just Tom, but Barbara was another story. Barbara Willis was an inescapable evil.

*A mother is the only woman you can trust?* Tom did not know whether to laugh, puke, or rip her lying tongue out of her mouth. The bitter-cold reality hurt like hell, and it penetrated Tom's heart like a blade. He had never experienced maternal love or caring. The sick and twisted things that she said and did were not out of love or caring like she said they were. They were nothing more than a sadistic expulsion of her own pain. Like venom from a viper's sac, she could only feel better after all of it was released into her victim.

Tom could smell the hatred that seeped from every pore of his mother's body. It hurt to realize that he had never seen anything good reflect back at him from her dead, black eyes. He may have never come to this realization if it had not been for the kindness that he saw in Sandy's eyes and heard in her quivering, yet compassionate voice. He had only met Sandy a few hours earlier, and under the worst circumstances imaginable, but in that short time, she

157

showed more kindness toward him than his own mother had shown him in all of his nineteen years.

*No wonder Mother can't hear the house and its beautiful scrolled woodwork talk to her.* Tom thought. The mansion was not *her* mansion. Maybe in title, yes. Her cruel, globular physical being could occupy it, but *it* would not occupy her. This mansion occupied souls, and she simply did not have one. He did not want to kill his mother in front of Sandy. She had already been through far too much because of him, and he could not stand the thought of her having the sight of his mother's blood and brain matter seared into her memory. He decided to do it upstairs, but first he had to figure out how to get her to waddle up the stairs, without having to first kill Sandy.

"Fine, Mother." Tom sighed. "I'll dig a hole in the woods for her body, but there's no way that I'll be able to see in this dark. I'll kill her in the morning, then I'll bury her. I promise. OK?"

Barbara's coal black eyes searched her son's face for any clue that he may be lying. He had never lied to her before, and quite frankly, she did not believe that he was smart enough to lie convincingly. "Well, the sooner the better. I need to get off my feet. They're killing me, so, I suppose that later will be alright. It doesn't look like she could get too far." She gave a satisfied smile as she motioned towards the flies that were landing on Sandy's buckshot mutilated leg. "Looks like you're going to have some pet maggots before too long." She laughed as she took the shotgun from Tom and ushered him upstairs so he could tend to her needs.

After a moment, Sandy heard the door to the upstairs closing. *It's all on you. You can do this. You gotta do this.* Sandy told herself. She did not know if she got through to Tom. She did not know if he was going to come back to help her, or if he was going to come back to kill her. She did not care. She was determined to pull the screws out of the wood that held the chains, then escape through the window.

## CHAPTER 25

Billy bit his fingernails down to the point of pain as he paced back and forth along the sidewalk at the end of his street. The sun was starting to go down quickly, but not quickly enough. Billy had his father's revolver tucked in the back waistband of his pants. *Come on, Ted. Hurry up and get here.* He said over and over to himself, hoping that Ted would pull up to get him before anyone saw him. Billy had never carried a gun before, and even though he had it tucked away with his shirt covering it, he believed that anyone who looked at him would somehow know that he was carrying it.

# OMINOUS WHISPERS

Billy stepped back into the shadow of a pine tree when he noticed the headlights of a car approaching. He hoped that it was Ted so they could just hurry up and go get Sandy from whoever he believes has her, and put an end to this craziness. The car slowed and pulled to the curb as it approached the corner. Billy stepped out from the shadow and breathed a sigh of relief when he saw that it was Ted, right on time, just as they had planned.

"Glad it's you." Billy said as he hopped into the passenger seat of Ted's El Camino. He took the gun out of the back of his pants and tucked it under his thigh on the seat of the car. "I was worried that a cop would drive by and wonder why I was standin' around on the street corner, then find out that I'm carryin' a gun."

Ted was too occupied by his own nervous thoughts to notice how stressed Billy was, or to even register what he was saying. *Is he the one who has her? Is she still alive? Is he gonna shoot at us? Are we gonna have to shoot him?* All of these questions, and more, raced through Ted's mind. The fear that he felt while waiting at home for it to get dark, was now replaced with a rush of mean, aggressive adrenaline. They were on their way. Their plan to rescue Sandy was in motion, and there was no way in hell that he would go home without her.

"Who do you think has her? - Where are we going?" Billy asked Ted as he wiped the sweat from his palms onto his jeans. "I mean, I gotta get mentally prepared, ya know?"

"Yeah...yeah, sorry Bill. OK. Remember when we stopped by Willis's place to pick up golf clubs? Ya know, when we went to the driving range with my family?"

"Yeah...I remember." Billy answered in a way that sounded more like a question, because he still was not sure what Ted was trying to say.

Ted turned and looked at Billy. "That house. That big-ass mansion. That's where I think she is. It was Willis's son in the bank today. He robbed the place, and he took Sandy, and that fat ass Willis did nothin' to stop him."

Billy was looking into eyes filled with determination and certainty. He was about to ask Ted if he was sure, but there was no need. The look in his best friend's eyes was assurance enough.

It was hard enough to find the long gravel driveway that led from the main road to the front door of the Willis mansion during the day, but it was damn near impossible to find it at night. *Evil prefers to hide in the dark,* Billy thought as Ted circled back around for a second drive down the main road to look for the entrance to the massive

162

estate. This time they found it, turned in and headed up the long driveway. Even though the mansion sat a good half-mile back from the main road, as soon as Ted pulled his car onto the property, he became concerned that someone would see the headlights, or hear the car on the gravel. They decided that it would be safest to drive on the grass as much as possible, and to keep the headlights off. When Ted turned the headlights off, they were enveloped in darkness, and could not even see the front of the car, let alone the driveway. It was a moonless night and they were away from the majority of the city lights, on a driveway flanked by thick forest on each side. Ted waited a moment to see if his eyes would adjust to the dark, but it was no use. He turned on the car's running lights and slowly drove toward the mansion, avoiding the noise of crushing gravel as much as possible.

As soon as the mansion came into sight, past the small hills and curves of the driveway, Ted and Billy decided that it would be safest to turn off the engine and walk along the tree line the rest of the way. Billy was about to tuck the revolver into his waistband again, but his intensifying fear made him decide to keep it at the ready in his hand. Ted brought a heavy, metal flashlight from home, and both boys, like always, had their pocket knives.

At the end of the tree line, to the right of the house, the grounds opened up into large areas of manicured lawn punctuated with a flower garden and gazebo. Far off to the left of the house, a tennis court, without a net, was barely visible. The gravel driveway ended in a large circle in front of the mansion. In the center of the circle there was a cement statue of an eagle, or some type of bird of prey, flanked by two curved cement benches and low shrubs. There were light fixtures aimed upward at the statue, but only one was working, and it was too dim to effectively light it up. Just to the left of the house, a tall, wrought iron, street light style lantern glowed, revealing a narrow, paved driveway that went off of the main gravel driveway circle, down the slope, toward the tennis court. There was also something else to the right of the tennis court, but it was too dark to see.

A light hung above the main entrance to the mansion, and a sconce illuminated a second smaller door which was also at the front of the mansion, but looked more like a servant's entrance. As Ted and Billy crept toward the mansion, they could see that the first floor looked completely dark, and the only light that they could see from the front of the mansion, came from a room on the second floor. As they got closer, they stayed to the right to avoid the lighted areas at the front of the mansion. Suddenly, Ted saw something. He put his arm out in front of Billy to stop him.

# OMINOUS WHISPERS

"Bill, look at the ground on the side of the house." Ted whispered, as he pointed ahead and off to their right.

"Hey, it looks like it might be a little light coming from a basement window." Billy squinted his eyes trying to get a clearer view.

"Yeah, I think it is. Let's head toward it. Our best shot at getting in will probably be through a basement window if they're big enough."

As they got closer, Billy said, "Cool, the windows don't have bars on em'!" Billy whispered. With each step, fear and dread was building up inside of him like a boiler with a stuck relief valve.

"Nobody's gonna have bars on their windows out here. We're not in the hood! Ted scoffed.

The boys got on their hands and knees and crawled as they approached the basement window. Billy tucked the gun back into his waistband, concerned that it might go off, crawling with it still in his hand. Ted laid flat on his belly, inched his face toward edge of the window and peeked in. A thump pounded through his chest like a kick from a mule. Ted gasped. He wanted to holler, but he knew better. He choked his emotions back down his throat. He took a quick scan through as much of the basement as he could see, then rolled on his side toward

Billy who was crouched behind him. Ted's voice cracked, and tears rolled down his face and across his stitched upper lip as he whispered to Billy. "It's Sandy! She's in there!"

OMINOUS WHISPERS

CHAPTER 26

Ted got up on his knees. "OK," He whispered. "I'm gonna try this window, and if it's locked, I'm gonna bust it out."

Instant terror rushed through Billy. He could hear his heart beat-swoosh, swoosh-in his ears. He grabbed Ted's shoulders and squeezed. There was enough light coming through the basement window for Billy to get a look at Ted's eyes. A chill ran up Billy's spine. Ted's eyes were wide with anxious glee *and* vengeful hatred. Scary eyes, like the guy at their school, who overdosed on mescaline - off the rails of a total manic episode in which caution and rational thought be damned. "Damn it, Ted! Wait!" Billy hissed. Is she alone?"

"Yeah, she's alone." Ted replied as fast as a radio announcer zipping through the fine print of an ad.

"If we just bust in there, she's not gonna know that it's us, she'll scream, and Giganto will come running. So we gotta take a second and think this through!" Billy said, still gripping Ted's shoulders.

Ted's eyes softened, and he nodded. "You're right, Bill. You're right. I don't know what I'd do without ya, brother. No one else would have my back and risk their life with me like you are. I pray to God that we get out of this, and don't get killed. I couldn't stand the thought of taking you down with me."

That was all that Billy had ever wanted. The feeling of being needed and valued, filled him with courage that welled up inside of him like lava building in a volcano. He scooted to the window and looked in. He could see that Sandy was standing, facing the window, and that she had both hands raised up to a low hanging rafter, and that chains were hanging down at her sides.

Billy sat back and looked at Ted. "I'm thinkin' that maybe you should tap on the window, just hard enough to get her attention. Let her see that it's you, but put your finger up to your mouth, ya know, like tellin' her to shush. Then we'll try to get the window open."

Ted nodded in agreement.

TAMMY GACH

CHAPTER 27

*Thank God they didn't think to turn that light bulb off before they left.* Sandy thought as she fought through her pain and steadied herself on her good leg. Her escape plan was playing through her head like a movie. When she got to the part where she would go through the pitch black woods toward the main road, to avoid the open view of the gravel driveway, she remembered something that she had seen last summer – Funny where your mind can take you when it is in overdrive.

She and Ted had been standing and talking on her front lawn when her neighbor's beagle, Missy, came running toward them, happy and excited like she had done dozens of times before. And, just like dozens of times before, when Sandy and Ted saw her coming, they called her over to play. "What's she dragging...?" Ted started to ask when they both realized that the little dog's intestines were out of her body and they were dragging through the dirt, grass and leaves. Even though she was tripping on the entrails with her back feet, she seemed blissfully unaware of the seriousness of her condition as she ran toward them. Turns out that the dog had been spayed a couple of days before, and the incision had dehisced - that is, it basically opened right back up instead of healing. Missy was taken back to the vet, who irrigated away the debris, sewed her back up with a different type of suture and put her on antibiotics. The little dog was fine, and seemed completely unfazed by the incident. In the past, whenever Sandy remembered the incident, she got weak in the knees. Tonight, however, the thought of the stoic little dog empowered her. *Missy could have probably jumped through this basement window, with her guts trailing behind her, if someone on the other side called her to play. So, don't think, just do, San. Just get the hell out of here.*

The rafter was not rotted quite as soft as it looked, but Sandy was making some progress in pulling the screws out. *Single focus...Keep going,* Sandy was telling herself when she heard the noise outside the basement window.

171

For a moment, she thought that she was hallucinating from blood loss, or stress. She could not believe what she was seeing. Ted was looking at her through that very window, with a shushing finger to his lips, and a flashlight to his face so that she could see that it was him.

Sandy's heart was beating so hard, and so fast, that she thought it might explode. She wanted to jump through that window, and run to Ted, dragging that entire fucking basement behind her by those damned chains. She feverishly began to work at the screws that held her chains to the rafter, as Ted slid silently through the unlocked window, and into the basement.

Ted ran to Sandy. They kissed each other's faces, wiping away tears, and shushing one another for fear of being discovered. Billy slid through the window, right behind Ted. Silent tears streamed down his face as his shaking hands went to work helping Ted to free the chains that held Sandy.

"I've almost got this one, Bill." Ted whispered, nodding his head toward the rafter and the chain that imprisoned Sandy's right arm. As he turned to look, Billy took a step back, and bumped an old window frame that was leaning against a stack of newspapers. Billy grabbed for the window as it fell, but it happened too fast. The glass panes shattered as the window hit the filthy cement

172

floor. The three cringed, and held their breath. They became as still as statues. Frozen in a moment of panic, they listened in silent terror, for footsteps or movement from upstairs. Hearing nothing, they got back to work on the chains.

Boom! Boom! Boom! Three thunderous crashes exploded on the staircase as Tom flew down the steps. The shock hit the three teens in an instant, and it hit them hard. Their worst fear had come to fruition. Ted and Sandy cringed - again. Every muscle in their bodies seized in momentary paralysis. Billy, who was no stranger to someone unexpectedly lunging at him, spun around and jumped back. "Shit!" he yelled, as nothing more than a startle reflex.

There he stood, the same hulking freak, the killer of innocent guinea pigs, who had stood next to the car staring at them the day that they came to pick up the golf clubs. At that moment, if Billy would have had the time to process a thought, rather than to just react on instinct, he would have been terrified. A deranged giant was growling at him through bared, yellow, clenched teeth. Sweat ran down Tom's round, pasty white face, and dripped from his protruding brow that hung like an awning over beady eyes that glowed red with rage.

# TAMMY GACH

Billy took one more step back, distancing himself from Ted and Sandy, he pulled his father's pistol from the back waistband of his jeans. It was too late. Tom caught a glimpse of the gun the second that Billy swung it around. Billy didn't even have time to aim. Tom leveled his sawed off shotgun, and howled like an animal – alone and dying in the dead of winter, as he blasted a hole through Billy's chest.

Rage tore through Ted. He charged, head down, at Tom like an enraged bull charges a matador. Tom did not see the freight train coming at him. His shot gun was still aimed at Billy's lifeless body, and his back was turned toward Ted and Sandy. Ted was a big guy, but even on his best day there would have been no way that he could knock Tom off his feet. But, a surprise attack from behind, fueled by a blinding blood red rage, sent Tom slamming, face first, to the ground. Tom's shotgun slid across the basement floor, out of his reach. Ted jumped to his feet, knowing that Tom would pin him and crush him if they fought on the ground.

Sandy ripped and pulled at her chains in a manic hysteria. It did not matter to her whether the chains ripped from the rafters, or her hands ripped from her arms, as long as she could break free. One friend was already dead, and she knew that Ted could only land so many punches on

174

# OMINOUS WHISPERS

Tom before the tables would turn, and Tom would swat and kill Ted as easily as he could kill a mosquito.

Tom stood up, undaunted by the punches and kicks that were raining down upon him. He could not hear Ted yelling at him, or Sandy screaming in terror. All he could hear were the voices. Too many voices at once, all of them telling him what to do. Women, yelling at him. First, one woman, then two. Their denigrating words, sharply pierced his brain and bounced around in his head like nails being shaken inside a rusty coffee can. Auditory hallucinations were ganging up on him as he charged, head first, into a complete psychotic break. Tom clawed at his ears until they were bloody. He wanted to rip them off of his head as the imagined verbal attack reached a deafening zenith.

"SHUT UP! ALL OF YOU, JUST SHUT UP!" He yelled. But they did not shut up. His mother, Sandy, the mansion – all of them – boring holes through his eardrums with their venomous words, slithering deep into his brain. *You're so stupid! Can't you see that you're doing it wrong! The evil has you now! You're just like your parents! Filthy male! You're just like your father! Ticka, ticka, ticka.* He had snapped, and there was no going back.

Sandy cried and screamed and fought even harder to get out of her chains, like a feral cat trying to escape from a trap. Tom turned his attention back to Ted, who was still punching him. Easily gaining the upper hand, he knocked Ted to the ground, and jumped on top of him. Tom wrapped both of his massive hands around Ted's throat, and began slamming the back of his skull into the concrete floor. Through the chaotic screams, cries, and brain-piercing voices, no one heard Barb's thunderous plodding on the basement stairs. No one saw her walk up behind Sandy and raise that damned blood encrusted bowling pin with both hands, and then bring it crashing down on the back of her skull. The blow made Sandy crumple, face down on the filthy mattress. The last thing she saw, was Ted's blood as it sprayed from the back of his head, and painted the floor, walls and rafters, with each slam against the ground – creating a sickening canvas of abstract expressionist art.

"See all the trouble you've caused, you trashy little whore!" Barb hissed and grunted as she struck the final, fatal blow to Sandy's skull.

Tom continued to slam the shattered, bloody remnants of Ted's head into the concrete. Drowning in a sea of psychotic rage, he just wanted the taunting voices in his head to stop. He had no idea that his mother was fifteen feet behind him, bludgeoning the last bit of life out of one of the only people who had ever tried to understand him.

## OMINOUS WHISPERS

Tired and out of breath, Tom let go of Ted's neck, letting his almost headless shoulders drop to the ground. Drenched in sweat, and spattered with blood, Tom crawled toward his shotgun that had been knocked out of his hand when Ted tackled him. He struggled to his feet, and turned to see his mother, standing next to Sandy's caved in skull. He slowly walked toward them, stopping to bend down and pick up the pistol that was still clutched in Billy's hand. At first, he thought that he was imagining it, but then he heard the snorts that came from the back of his mother's throat, as she gasped to catch her breath. This was reality. Vulgar, bloody reality.

As Tom stood there, surveying the carnage, he realized that there was only one woman's voice in his head that was still taunting him. His mother's. Sandy's voice was still there, but it was not taunting him. Sandy's voice was still in his head, and he realized that, all along, her voice had been telling him, *it's not your fault, Tom. Your brother, Jeff wants to get to know you – we're friends.*

"SHUT UP!" Tom yelled at the wicked voice. Startled, Barbara dropped the bowling pin on the mattress. Tom took one last look at the vicious, cunning predator who had given birth to him. Then he raised the shotgun, and blasted his mother's face, and most of her skull, right off of her body.

177

## CHAPTER 28

There was silence. The voices, the whispering, the pain – all gone. Tom had forgotten what quiet sounded like. The voices had teased and provoked him, but now he was afraid. He was afraid of the silence that had a sound all its own.

He looked around at the lifeless bodies, and the blood – all that blood. The thick smell of blood and gunpowder irritated his nose and throat. Tom rolled his mother's faceless carcass off of Sandy. He kept pushing and rolling it until it was off the mattress, and on the cold, dirty floor.

With his giant shoulders slumped, and his head hung low, Tom laid the guns down, and sat on the mattress next to Sandy. He cried as he gently brushed Sandy's long blood soaked hair from her dusky face. Her eyes were open, and still reflected the terror that she felt during her last moments of life. He tried to close them, like he had seen done a hundred times on television, but it did not work. They just kept opening. He lumbered up the stairs, and got a blanket from the linen closet. He covered Sandy, as if she were sleeping, then he laid down beside her and cried himself to sleep.

TAMMY GACH

# CHAPTER 29

August 25, 1978

The ghastly image of being handcuffed and forced into the back of a police cruiser, while Barbara gleefully watched, jarred Alfred awake. *Oh, thank God it was only a nightmare!* He thought. After a fitful night, he was surprised that he had fallen asleep. Alfred sat up in bed, and looked at the alarm clock on the nightstand. The sun was just starting to come up, and he gave a deep sigh of relief to find that it was still early. He looked at Liz, sound asleep next to him. Before he could stand up and head to

180

the bathroom, Alfred winced and gripped his chest. He felt a sinking disappointment when the pain subsided as quickly as it came. *A heart attack would be easier,* He thought, as he wondered which of the two things that he knew were coming today, would be worse – Going home to face Tom and Barbara, and probably the kidnapped Sandy, or how Liz and Jeff would react when they discover that his bank had been robbed yesterday, and Jeff's friend had been kidnapped, and he had not mentioned a thing to them about it.

Alfred was relieved that Jeff, and then Liz had fallen asleep without seeing or hearing the news. Ripping the cord clean out of the back of the television, while they were out of the room, had worked. Now all he had to do was to leave the house before they woke up. The longer he could avoid conflict, the better. He washed his face, shaved, and put on some fresh clothes. "I have a ton of stuff to do at the bank today, so I'm going in early." He whispered in Liz's ear. Still sleepy, she turned toward him, gave him a kiss, and drifted back to sleep.

The chest pain gripped him each time he thought about going to the mansion. He did not really want to know what kind of hell was playing out over there, but he turned his car radio to the local news channel anyway. It did not take long for the top story to come on. This time, the pain gripped his chest with a vengeance. He pulled the car over

181

while he caught his breath. He did not expect to hear the latest breaking news – "Two teenage boys, known to be close friends of the young woman who was kidnapped from the bank on Thursday, are now also missing…" Now he really did not want to go to the mansion, but he knew that he could not avoid it forever. He considered going to the bank, collecting all of the money from the safe, and just disappearing. It was something to think about.

Very few things could quell Alfred's appetite, so he decided to stop at a restaurant for breakfast, and take some time to consider his options.

OMINOUS WHISPERS

CHAPTER 30

The sound of flies buzzing around his head woke Tom that morning. Sandy's cold, stiff body was beside him, eyes still open with the same terrified gaze. Tom remembered his mother's heartless, taunting words when he looked at Sandy's buckshot riddled leg. The evil one was right. Sandy's leg was a bubbling sea of hatching maggots.

For the first time in his life, no one was telling Tom what to do, or how to do it. It was what he had always wanted, but he soon realized that it posed a real problem – now, he was not sure what to do. He did not want to go to jail, so after grueling consideration, he decided how he could make it all disappear.

Tom stepped out the front door into the warm summer sun. He looked around, and wondered how the two guys got to his house last night, because the green van was the only vehicle in sight. He went back down to the basement, and checked their blood stained pockets for car keys. He found a single house key in the front pocket of Billy's jeans, and a keyring with house and car keys in Ted's front pocket. He took Ted's keys with him as he drove the green work van down the long, twisting driveway to look for a car that they may have parked there. It did not take long to find the gold El Camino, parked on the grass, next to the driveway.

Tom got into the El Camino, and moved the seat back as far as it could go. He grumbled to himself as he drove the car back up to the mansion, because he did not like driving a car that sat so low to the ground. He wondered if he preferred the work van simply because he had never driven anything else. Something to ponder another time. Right now, he had work to do.

Tom loosely wrapped the bloody corpses in blankets, and carried them up the stairs, one by one, saving the big, backbreaking one for last. He took them out the solarium door, at the back of the mansion, where he had parked

## OMINOUS WHISPERS

Ted's El Camino on the grass, before the steep slope. At first, he thought about throwing the bodies in the back of the El Camino, and then pushing it down the slope and into the pond at the bottom, but that just would not work. The bodies might float, so he put the three teens inside the car. Tom groaned and huffed under the weight of his mother. When he finally made it to the car, he found that no matter how hard he pushed, she just would not fit in the front seat with the others, and the El Camino didn't have a back seat. He let her drop onto the grass next to the car. He wiped away the sweat that was stinging his eyes and tickling his nose as it dripped off of it, and then he sat down to rest, and to consider his next move.

The thought of having to do more strenuous work, made Tom feel nauseated. It was not just that. The strain of carrying Barbara up the stairs, started his rectal pain and bleeding again. Tom took a deep breath, put the car in neutral, closed the windows and doors, and with a big huff, pushed the car down the hill and watched as it slowly bobbed and descended in the deep water of the murky pond. He turned, walked past his mother, still on the grass wrapped in blankets, and headed down the gravel driveway for the long, painful walk to get the work van.

He wished there was another way, but if there was, he could not think of it. Tom loved the green work van, but not only did his mother need to end up in the drink with the other three, but he also knew that sooner or later someone would recognize the green van as the one used in the bank robbery and kidnapping. *Ticka, ticka, ticka,* the combination of sadness and anxiety was boring through the center of Tom's gut as he pictured Sandy and his van, both stuck in the silt and decaying vegetation at the bottom of the pond. But, it had to be done. So, with the strength that came from his seething anger, he threw his mother into the back of the van.

The sound of crushing gravel on the driveway startled Tom as he was just about to push the van down the hill. He had completely forgotten that Jeff promised to come by, around nine a.m. Tom started to cry and shake, panicked that Jeff would hate him for what happened to Sandy.

Jeff got out of his car and rushed over to Tom. He could see that Tom was shaken, and that his face, pants, and the shirt that was balled up in his hand were all covered with blood.

"Oh Jeez, Tom! What happened? Are you hurt?" Jeff's mouth hung open, and his face turned ghostly white as he stood looking at his half-brother.

# OMINOUS WHISPERS

"You're gonna hate me!" Tom trembled and sobbed, so distraught, that Jeff had a hard time understanding him. "I just met you, and now you're gonna hate me!"

Jeff led Tom over to a small retaining wall, and had him sit down. Jeff could not imagine why Tom was so upset that he would not even make eye contact.

"I'm not gonna hate you, Tom. Look at me. It's OK." Jeff said as he assured Tom, leaning forward to get Tom to look at him.

Tom looked at Jeff, and blew his nose on the bloody shirt in his hand. Tears continued to stream down Tom's face as he shook his head and said, "I don't even know where to begin."

"Well, just start at the beginning, I guess." Jeff said as he gave Tom's sweaty shoulder a squeeze of encouragement.

"OK." Tom nodded, then started to tell his brother the most ugly, horrific story that he had ever heard. "It's really been going on since I was born, but the really, really bad shit that led to this, happened when my mother got those pictures of your mother and our father..."

Tom told the story in nauseating detail, while Jeff sat and listened in incredulous silence, until Tom reached the

187

part where he kidnapped Sandy to show his father that he was serious and he had had enough.

"WHAT! Where...where is she?" Jeff jumped up and hollered, the pressure of his blood pounded hot in his temples.

"Ticka, ticka, ticka." Tom slid down the retaining wall, and sat, rocking back and forth on the grass, his mind locked in a trance of guilt and sorrow.

Crying, and barely able to speak, Jeff forced himself to ask, "Is she alive?"

Tom shook his head, and barely audible, he squeaked out "No."

Jeff fell to his hands and knees, sobbing and pulling at the grass. He looked at Tom, and with tears streaming down his swollen, beet red face, he asked, "You killed her?"

"No! I was going to get her out of here and take her home, you know, after we talked and all, and she told me that she knew you - I was so sorry for pulling her into my bullshit, and I was going to sneak her out when my mother was sleeping, because she told me I couldn't let her go, that I had to kill her - then two guys broke in, and one had a gun – I didn't know who they were – cops or maybe they were trying to rescue her, but when he pulled the gun out, I just went crazy - my head just went crazy, and my fat bitch of a mother killed her while I was fighting with the other guy - it wasn't me, but it was all my fault!" Gasping sobs and snot sucking sniffles were the only punctuations in Tom's rambling answer to his brother's question. Then he took a long, deep breath, and looked at Jeff. "I killed my mother, and the other two guys, but I didn't kill Sandy – I swear to you!"

There were no words exchanged. For a moment that felt like forever to both of them, they just sat on the grass, sobbing and rocking in agony.

Jeff's head reeled as he tried to make sense of it all. *Alfred didn't mention a damn thing about Sandy being kidnapped from the bank. That's how the power cord got pulled clean out of the TV! He didn't want us to see it on the news! That lousy son of a bitch! Was he protecting Tom, or himself? Did he even know that it was Tom who was kidnapping Sandy from the bank?* Foamy spit filled Jeff's mouth from the nausea that he felt when his mind came to the most obvious conclusion – the one thing that was certain. *Alfred wasn't worried about protecting Sandy. She might still be alive if he would have went home that day instead of hiding under my mom's wing!*

TAMMY GACH

"Did Alfred see you, and know that it was you in the bank that day? Did he see you take Sandy?" Jeff asked. Anger was starting to replace his sadness.

"I had on a mask, but he knew it was me. I could see it in his eyes. He just shut the entire stinking thing out. He just let it all happen, the abuse, the robbery, the kidnapping, just so he wouldn't have to deal with me and my crazy mother, and his damn reputation that he always bellyaches about!" Tom said, shaking his head, his face buried in his hands.

Jeff slammed his fist into the palm of his hand. It pissed him off, but it did not surprise him at all.

"I know that you hate me now, so if you want to shoot me, I don't blame you." Tom continued to look down at the grass as he worked to pull the pistol out of his front pants pocket, and then hand it to Jeff.

"Put that damn thing away! And, no. I don't hate you. All that shit that your mother did to you, and that fucking asshole of a father ignoring it. Shit, Tom, I'd have done the same thing as you, but probably a lot sooner!"

Tom dropped the pistol on the grass, next to him. Both boys sat in silence, except for the sniffling, and wondered what to do nex

# OMINOUS WHISPERS

## CHAPTER 31

The sound of gravel crunching beneath car tires, pulled Jeff and Tom out of their stupors of sadness, fear and disbelief. Alfred had finished both of the breakfasts that he had ordered while he garnered enough courage to go home and face whatever he would find waiting for him. He had decided, after the second 'meat lovers' omelet, that he would deny knowing that the robber – kidnapper was his own son. Clearly the police would see that Tom was not right in the head, so why would they believe any stories that he might tell them about how horrible his parents were? No way would they take the word of a mentally deficient, monstrously huge nineteen year old, over the word of a well-respected banker. Once again, Alfred Willis had consoled himself.

191

# TAMMY GACH

Alfred pulled the Cadillac around the circular drive, nearest to the main entry to the mansion. He smiled and wiped the ever-present perspiration from his brow and face with his handkerchief. *Good. No cop cars. That's a good sign!"* He thought. He didn't notice Tom and Jeff, sitting on the grass at the far west end of the house, until he dislodged himself from his car, and the boys stood up.

He squinted his eyes, wondering if he really was seeing Jeff standing there with Tom. It was the last place that he had ever expected to see Jeff, and seeing him so far out of his normal context, confused Alfred at first. Confusion and disbelief quickly became a chill of terror that ran up his spine, the moment he saw blood on Tom, and the look of burning hatred on both of their tear streaked faces.

Jeff and Tom approached Alfred, and stopped about ten feet away from him. Alfred just stood there, eyes wide, saturating his clothing with the sweat that was pouring from him. He knew that anything he would say would somehow be wrong at that moment. Oh, what he would not give for the comfortable safety of Liz, and her soothing cookies and wine.

"Why weren't you ever here? How come you were never ever here to protect me?" Tom yelled at his father.

## OMINOUS WHISPERS

Alfred gasped, took a step back, and slowly raised his hands. Jeff looked at Tom, standing next to him, and realized that Tom had picked up the gun from the grass when he saw his father's car pull up.

Tom waived the gun wildly while he continued to yell at Alfred. "You knew what she was doing to me! You knew that she was hurting me and making me have sex with her – BECAUSE YOU WEREN'T HERE!"

Alfred shook to his core with fear. It was not like the last time that Tom waived a gun around at the bank. No. This was not just a show of frustration. There was blood on Tom's hands, pants and shoes. Hate glared from his wild, red eyes, and spit sprayed from between bared yellow teeth, like a rabid demon dog. No. Alfred knew that this was the point of no return, and he began to cry, terrified to find out where the blood, and the pistol had come from.

"Tom, Buddy." Jeff quietly said, putting his hand on Toms shoulder, and gesturing toward the gun with his head. "Why don't you let me hold that for right now? I'll give it back, I promise."

Tom would have done anything for his brother, the only person who had ever been completely there for him. "Sure Jeff." He said so calmly that he seemed like a totally different person than the one who had been yelling with such ferocity, just a moment before.

A trembling sigh of relief burst from Alfred when Tom handed the gun over to Jeff.

"SHE..." Tom started to yell at Alfred again, but Alfred was not about to have any of it now that Tom wasn't pointing a gun at him. Alfred put his hand up, and shook his head, telling Tom to stop talking. He was trying to look sympathetic, but the only one Alfred was fooling, was himself. His sudden smug confidence oozed from him like pus from a boil as he held out his hand for the gun, and walked toward Jeff.

"You stop right there and let him finish what he has to say to you! You aren't gonna fucking run away from the truth, this time!" Jeff yelled, not needing to point the gun at their father. Pointing his finger was enough to stop Alfred, and to shut him up.

Tom felt a mix of pride and love for his brother, and hatred for their father, that was almost too painful and confusing to bear.

"She raped me! She rammed a bowling pin up my ass with a hammer! Do you know how that feels? Would you like to know how that feels you selfish mother fucker?" Tom hissed at his father. The heat of his anger raged so hot, that Jeff could feel it, while standing next to Tom, radiating from him like a furnace.

The blood drained from Alfred's round, red face, then he leaned forward and puked. Jeff looked at the vomit that dripped from his father's silk tie, and the custom made shirt that strained to cover his pot belly. The fear that he might be sodomized with the bowling pin, at the hands of his son, as a form of revenge, curdled Alfred's blood. Daddy Dearest did not give a rat's ass about the horrors that Tom had been put through. The prospect of that happening to *him*, scared the two breakfast's right out of him.

Alfred spat the taste of vomit from his mouth the best that he could. He could see that the red glare of rage was fading from Tom's eyes, and that he was calming down a bit. Alfred figured that telling his story and getting his anger out made Tom feel better, but he was not sure. Maybe Tom was feeling better, or maybe it was just the calm before the storm. Either way, he did not want to say anything that might set him off again.

Alfred's mind was still in fast forward, like a rat fleeing a sinking ship, thinking through every angle of the story that he would tell police to protect himself. He really needed to know if the blood on his son came from Sandy.

TAMMY GACH

"There's a lot of blood on you, Tom." Alfred said softly, poorly feigning concern.          "Is Sandy, the bank teller, dead?"

"They all are." Tom said in an eerily calm voice that chilled Alfred.

Shock, like an unexpected jolt of electricity, surged through Jeff's body. He should have known, and he did, but the confirmation of his biggest fear hit Jeff harder than he could have imagined. His father, the man that his mother loved, *did* know that Tom was the man in the bank that day. He did know that Tom was so ignored and abused, that he snapped just to get some attention. He did know that it was Tom who abducted Sandy at gunpoint. He knew all along, and he did nothing to help her. He sacrificed that beautiful, sweet, young girl, simply to protect his money and his reputation.

Jeff could feel every pulse point in his body, pound like a bass drum. His vision turned to a dark fuzzy haze, and he thought that he might pass out.

"They're all dead?" Alfred's jowls jiggled as his jaw dropped, and his eyes were wide in a dumbfounded gaze. You mean those two boys – her friends – that Ted and Billy, the ones that I heard on the radio are missing? You

196

mean they're dead too?" Alfred wretched and coughed, fighting the urge to vomit again.

Before Tom could answer, Jeff shouted. "Wait! Did you just say that Sandy's friend Ted, and another kid are missing?" He began to hyperventilate. Jeff dropped to his knees, wrapped his arms over his head, and rocked back and forth. He had not even considered that he may have known the two guys that Tom said he shot when they broke in.

Alfred did not respond, but his silence said it all. Tom started to cry, and bent down next to Jeff. "I'm sorry! Did you know those guys? Oh God, Jeff. I'm so sorry! I'm such a fuck-up!" Tom began pounding his fists against the sides of his own head in a fit of self-loathing.

Jeff stood up, and pulled on his brother's arm. "Come on, Tom. Stop that. Stand up. It's not your fault. You said he had a gun. You couldn't have known."

Fear and confusion were taking their toll on Alfred. A deflating sigh, long and slow, came from his nose, and he hung his head, resting his chin rolls on his chest. *I don't give a shit what happened here, or to who, or even what's going to happen to me. I'm hotter than hell, soaked in sweat, and I reek of vomit. I just want it to end!* He told himself.

TAMMY GACH

Jeff hated what Tom had done, and he wanted to hate Tom for doing it, but he could not. Just like the nicest dog in the world will bite if it is cornered and hurt, people are no different, and Jeff knew that. His brother was pushed to the edge of sanity. He held on for a long time, but he had finally been pushed too hard, and too far, and he fell over that edge.

Sickened and angered to his core, Jeff raised the pistol and aimed it at Alfred. "You reacted, Tom – in a bad way – but in the only way that you knew how. You didn't know," Jeff said to Tom. "But he did!" He gestured toward their father.

Alfred raised his head and saw that Jeff had the gun pointed at him. Once again, the blood drained from his face, and drops of sweat landed on his shirt, as he listened.

"He knew that you had Sandy, and he did nothing to help her. He knew what your mom was doing to you, and he did nothing to help you, either. This useless, cowardly prick is the one to blame!" Jeff jabbed the gun forward with every word of condemnation, as if it were a sword, meant to cut their father with each jab. "He could have stopped this whole damned mess before it ever even got started! He ran away from your mom instead of getting the psycho the help she needed for her mental shit…"

# OMINOUS WHISPERS

Pulling at his necktie, Alfred cleared his throat, making the wet with phlegm, percolating gurgle that Jeff had grown to hate. He started to say something, but instead, just shook his head slightly and lowered it again. Alfred finally looked up, just in time to see Jeff pull the trigger, sending a bullet right between his, once bright, tear-filled blue eyes.

The saying is true – *The bigger they are, the harder they fall*. From ten feet away, both Tom and Jeff felt the quake beneath their feet when their father hit the ground. They stood in stunned silence for a minute that felt like an hour, then Jeff gave the gun back to Tom, just as he had promised.

Wait here for a minute, Tom said. Jeff watched him as he walked around the side of the mansion. Tom went to get the green van. He backed it out, away from the grassy slope, and over to Alfred's lifeless body.

"I didn't want to have to carry his fat ass to the van, so I brought it to him." Tom said, as he opened the back doors of the van.

"Shit!" Jeff gasped, stumbling backward and covering his nose when he looked into the van. He did not expect to see, or smell a huge, bloated, rotting dead woman,

199

partially wrapped in a bloody blanket, with half of her head blown off.

"Oh, yeah. Meet my mother." Tom said when he saw Jeff's reaction. "I was just about to push the van down the hill, into the pond out back, when I heard you pull up. Now I can throw him in there too."

"Karma." Jeff said with a slight grin and chuckle. He was surprised that he was able to laugh, after just killing his own father. He wondered, for the briefest moment, if he was an evil person, deep down inside. *Only a real sicko would be able to laugh so easily, right after shooting his father between the eyes,* he thought, but the irony was too much to keep to himself. "Dear Old Dad won't be able to escape 'Nut Job' now." He said to Tom. "The bastard's gonna have to share an underwater crypt with her now!"

"Well, they deserve each other, as far as I'm concerned." Tom said, with a 'job well done' nod of his head.

"Shit! I thought I was strong." Jeff said, surprised by how he nearly dropped Alfred as they struggled to stuff him into the van with Barbara's buckshot riddled carcass.

Finally, the van was back at the edge of the slope to the pond. Jeff worried about what they would do if the van got stuck, and didn't completely submerge. "Is the pond deep enough to cover the van?" He asked Tom. Jeff shuddered. It hit him at that moment that the bottom of the pond is most likely where Sandy and the two boys already were. They were not in the van, and Tom did not say he still needed to put them in the van. Jeff did not ask. He could not bear to know.

Tom hesitated, and felt a twinge of guilty sadness when he saw the look in his brother's eyes. He knew that he was probably wondering about Sandy, so he lowered his head, and simply said, "Yeah. It's plenty deep enough." He hated that Jeff was hurting so badly for something that he had done, and he hoped that the heart ripping pain that he was feeling for hurting Jeff and Sandy, would stay with him forever. He felt that he deserved at least that much.

# CHAPTER 32

Unceremoniously, they pushed the van, and watched as it rolled down the hill, and slowly submerged into the murky water.

OMINOUS WHISPERS

CHAPTER 33

A splash of hot coffee landed on Detective Mark Baker's shirt. In his frustration, he slammed his *World's Best Dad* mug down on his desk a bit too hard.

"Damnit!" He grumbled as he stood up.

"Rough morning?" Another detective asked, as he tossed a box of tissues to Baker.

"Yeah." He sighed. "I've been trying to get ahold of Alfred Willis all morning – you know – the guy whose bank was robbed. Guess I'll head over to his house, and see if he's there. A couple of fucking questions that he coulda answered over the phone, if he'd just pick up the damned thing!" Baker complained.

When Detective Baker pulled his cruiser up to the mansion, he noticed that Willis' Cadillac was parked in the driveway. *Good.* He thought, until he noticed two young men walk out from behind the mansion. As soon as Tom and Jeff saw the car, they stopped cold in their tracks. After twenty years on the force, Baker could smell it when someone had something to hide, and those two reeked of it. He expected them to run, but they just stood there, their eyes wide with panic. As he approached Tom and Jeff, Baker noticed the blood spatter that covered the front of Tom's pants and boots. *Corduroy pants and heavy boots in ninety degree weather? OH SHIT!* Detective Baker pulled his gun the instant that he remembered that the people at the scene of the bank robbery and kidnapping told him that the perpetrator was a huge man wearing brown cords and Frye Brand boots.

"Hands in the air! Hands in the air NOW! Get down on your knees – both of you, and keep those hands up!" He yelled. Detective Baker reached his hand around to the back of his belt, and was relieved to find that he did have two pairs of handcuffs attached to his belt.

"Down on the ground! On your belly, both of you! Hands behind your head!" Detective Baker ordered. He cuffed Tom and Jeff, and then said, "Get up." He pulled on Jeff's arm to help him up. Gravel was stuck to the sweat on the side of his face. "You too, big boy!" He said to Tom, pulling on his arm to help him up. Tom rolled and grunted, but he needed his hands to push himself up from the ground. Baker was not about to un-cuff him because, he thought, *This huge-ass, mother fucker looks strong enough to wrap my gun around my throat if he wanted to.*

It was clear that Tom was not trying to resist arrest, he was simply too big to maneuver himself, and too heavy to lift without help. Baker put Jeff in the back of the car, and had Tom stay where he was, until back-up arrived.

# CHAPTER 34

At the police station, Tom and Jeff were placed in separate rooms for interrogation. Tom explained everything – in detail – that led up to his fateful decision to rob his father's bank. It was not until he got to the part about kidnapping Sandy, that he showed any remorse. Tears began to roll down his rounded cheeks. "I'd do anything to take it back." He cried. "I'd trade my life for Sandy's in a heartbeat, if God would let me."

Tom and Jeff's stories were identical from the point of Jeff showing up, until Detective Baker arrived – except for one thing. Jeff admitted to shooting his father, helping

## OMINOUS WHISPERS

Tom load him into the van, and helping him push it into the pond. Tom, on the other hand, took credit for all of it, telling the police that Jeff did not show up at Knob Hill until everyone was already dead at the bottom of the pond.

TAMMY GACH

PART III

CHAPTER 35

AUGUST 24, 2009

**THIRTY-ONE YEARS LATER**

"Fried, fried, fried!  People even want their bacon and sausage links deep fried!"  Pete smirked at his twin brother Nick as they worked side by side in the tiny, crowded diner.

# OMINOUS WHISPERS

"Yep. Heart attack on a plate." Nick Davis patted his dad on the shoulder as he brought up another case of eggs from the back cooler. "Hey Pop, if you ever think about changing the name of this place, that'd be a good one. Heart Attack on a Plate!"

"Hey, knock it off you guys! This place bought your diapers when you were babies, and it's bought you everything since! But, smart-asses, since it's your birthday today I'm gonna let some of your funny-guy comments slide!" Their father faked a scolding as he manned the grill with a finesse that came from forty years of doing the job that felt he was born to do.

"Yeah Dad, we know that you and Grandpa worked your asses off to build this place." Nick said.

"Damn right we did!"

"Aw, come on Dad." Pete Davis grinned as he bobbed and weaved, throwing a couple of pulled punches at his dad. "You know that Nick and I love this place. We only joke around because we find that humor helps the grease splatter blisters on our forearms heal faster!"

"Yeah, sure. You love it enough to want to leave me here while you two go off and start your hoity-toity snob restaurant." Lou Davis, a tough, weathered ex-Marine with thick white hair and a heart of gold, looked over the frames of his dime-store reading glasses at his sons. It was the same stern, no-nonsense look that used to quiet his boys right down when they were young, but now, it was the look that evoked a deeply secure feeling of paternal love in his sons. Lou studied Nick's eyes for a moment. Of the two boys, Nick was the more sensitive one, so he wanted to make sure that his son did not take his comments seriously.

Growing up, Pete was the kind of kid who blended into the background – never the hero, never the villain – just a happy-go-lucky guy. Nick, on the other hand, was altruistic to a fault. He had an insatiable need to prove himself. As Lou watched his sons grow, he would sometimes think back to his service in the jungles of Viet Nam. He lost half of his right foot – thanks to those damned jungles – not from a bullet, or grenade, or even one of those bouncing Betty's – but because his feet were wet for three months straight – never dry – not even for a minute. Lou said a lot of prayers of thanks over the years that his sons were born into a time in which they weren't sent off to war. Pete would have been fine, Lou thought, but Nick would have jumped at every opportunity to put himself in danger to save others. He would have gotten his damned head shot off. Now, after years of trying to convince Nick that the diner would survive just fine without him and his brother, Lou finally got through to his son. Now, Nick and Pete were making plans to follow their dreams and start their own restaurant. The last thing Lou wanted to do, was to send his kid into a guilt trip, from too much kidding him about leaving.

Just as Nick gave a hesitant chuckle to relieve his father's obvious worries, the sound of screeching tires and smashing metal was so close and abrupt that the people in the diner jumped and pulled their hands up to their heads in a reflex of self-protection. "Dad! Take over the grill!" Nick shouted as he leaped over the counter and ran out the door. At the intersection in front of the diner, Nick saw the left front wheel of a semi-truck completely inside of what had once been a silver convertible. The truck driver jumped down from the cab of his truck. "I couldn't stop! Oh shit! I couldn't stop!" He repeated over and over as he collapsed to his hands and knees in a fit of despair. He was not hurt, but he could not bring himself to look inside the car.

Nick ran to the car. He could see that there was no way he could access the passenger side, so he ran around the front to the driver's side. Nick's first glimpse inside the car caused a thud in the center of his chest as if he had been kicked by a mule. He could see a person with blood soaked hair trying to talk and move in the one tiny un-smashed portion of the car that remained. That sight, along with the sickening stench of burning electrical wires, gasoline and

211

blood snapped him into a mind-set of singly focused, calm control over the situation. He expected the driver's side door to be jammed, so he pulled hard to open it. It flung open easily, causing him to fall backwards on the pavement. A right hand, severed at the wrist, rolled out and landed between his legs. Nick ripped off his apron and searched with his hands through the tight confines of the car for the arm that was missing a hand. He could not see most of the driver's body because of the semi-truck tire that was parked in her lap. His hand came to rest in a warm pool of blood. The blood-lubricated arm slipped from his hand as he tried to pull it toward him. He knew that he would have to work quickly or the woman would bleed to death. He gripped her arm tightly, sinking his fingernails into her flesh to get a good grip. He managed to pull the arm toward him. The open wrist sprayed him with blood. He tightly tied the strings of his apron around the stump of the arm as a tourniquet to stop the bleeding. His tunnel vision focus was broken when he heard the woman moan "Ow!" She was alive and looking at him. Her cut forehead was scrunched into an angry frown as if to say "What the hell are you doing to me!"

"You're going to be OK, Miss. The ambulance is on its way. I'm right here, and I'm not leaving you." Nick smiled softly.

# OMINOUS WHISPERS

Her look of anger transformed into one of weakness and confusion. "An ambulance? I'm quite certain that I don't need an ambulance!" Her voice nearly inaudible as she worked to speak through the blood and thick saliva that filled her mouth.

Pete and the rest of the people from the diner began to gather. Nick picked up the severed hand and handed it to his brother. "Put this in a plastic bag, then pack the bag in ice before the ambulance gets here! Maybe they'll be able to reattach it." Pete nodded, steeling himself to do as his brother asked, without puking or passing out.

It seemed like an hour had gone by as Nick kneeled on the pavement next to the woman trapped in the wreckage of her car, but it had only been a few minutes. He heard at least two sirens in the distance as he stroked her blood-soaked hair. "Stay awake now. You're going to be just fine, but YOU HAVE TO STAY AWAKE!"

Two police cars, quickly followed by an ambulance and a fire truck pulled up to the intersection. Pete thought that his shaking legs would give out as he ran from the diner toward the first officer on the scene. He was as white and clammy as raw pizza dough as he quickly handed the ice-packed hand to the police officer.

The cop looked at Pete in momentary confusion. "What's this?"

"A hand. My brother said to pack it in ice."

"Oh...shit." The police officer's jaw muscles rippled as he clenched his teeth together. "What hospital are we going to?" he asked the paramedics who were already tending to the woman as the firemen cut through the twisted metal to free her.

"St. John's is the closest trauma center."

"OK. I'm going to send an officer ahead to the hospital with this hand..."

"Her hand is severed?" The paramedic's jaw fell open and his round face flushed as this new piece of information hit him.

"I was able to reach in and stop the bleeding. I used my apron as a tourniquet. She's been conscious and talking a bit. I don't think there's anyone else in the car." The deep, calm voice came from the athletically built, tall, blood-soaked man who had been kneeling next to the victim when they had arrived.

After the car was cut open, the freed woman was placed on a back board with her head immobilized. Her blood pressure was dangerously low due to hypovolemic shock

214

from blood loss, so the paramedic did not waste time trying to find a vein for an IV. He popped an intraosseous cannula for fluids into the tibia of her left leg. They looked and were relieved to discover that she was the only one in the car. If someone had been in the passenger seat, they would have been completely crushed. As they put her into the back of the ambulance, one of the paramedics turned to Nick and said "If she lives, it'll be in a big part because of you."

"Pop, I'm going to follow the ambulance to the hospital." Nick's head was still turned in the direction of the ambulance that had just sped off. He could not shake the feeling that he still had more to do to help the woman.

"No son. Come on. You're covered in blood. She's in good hands. Lou put his arms around both of his sons and gave their shoulders a squeeze as they stood on the sidewalk in front of the diner. "I am so proud of you guys. Not many people could have jumped in and did what you did to help that gal."

"All I did was what Nick told me to do, without passing out, which I still might do." Pete said, able to muster only a slight half-face grin.

"I gotta go dad. I'll wash up and change my clothes first, but I just need to."

His son was a man of strong conviction with a steel will. Lou knew that he would be wasting his breath to tell him that he was not needed at the hospital, so he simply smiled and gave an affirming nod.

The crowd dispersed and the last news crew left the scene. Lou and Pete closed up the diner early, and headed straight to Mc Govern's pub to wash away their experience with as much bourbon as it would take.

OMINOUS WHISPERS

CHAPTER 36

Nick shook his head to clear the fog, then he glanced down at the speedometer. He eased up on the gas pedal when he saw that he was going twenty miles per hour over the speed limit. His black Ford Explorer must have been on auto pilot, he thought, when he realized that he was almost at the hospital, but had no recollection of the drive there. He pulled into the visitor parking lot for the emergency department, and suddenly realized that he did not know the name of the girl that he had helped. *I suppose it doesn't matter.* He thought. *How many car accident victims with a severed hand could have possibly come to emergency via an ambulance, within the last hour?*

"Can I help you, Sir?" The woman behind the information desk asked, in a voice that sounded at least as distracted as Nick had felt during his auto pilot drive. *Lights are on, but no one's home.* He thought as he listened to her tap the longest, most ornate fingernails that he had ever seen, and huff as if she were being put out by his presence.

"Yes ma'am. A young woman was just brought in a little while ago, by ambulance. Bad car accident..."

"Surgery." She said, before Nick could finish his sentence.

"Surgery?" Nick asked, assuming that the woman meant that she was in surgery, wherever that was.

"Down this hall, then take the elevator to the second floor. The surgical waiting lounge is right there across from the elevator. They got coffee up there. We don't got no coffee down here!" She complained, then she tuned him out and adeptly used her freakishly long fingernails to start texting on her sequined bedazzled cell phone.

Nick entered the surgical lounge. It was a pleasant enough place, for a hospital, anyway. There were plenty

218

of comfortable looking chairs, two televisions, the coffee that the fingernail lady had mentioned, some bored, and some worried looking people, waiting for loved ones who were in surgery, and an a smiling elderly woman wearing a blue blazer with the word "Volunteer" embroidered on it. *Oh, good.* Nick thought. *Someone who **wants** to be here to help people!*

"May I help you, Sir?" The grandmotherly woman asked.

"Yes ma'am. This may sound strange - I don't know her name, but I'm here to find out how the young woman from the car accident is. The one with the severed hand." Nick winced as he asked. The little elderly woman seemed too sweet to hear such horrific words as, "severed hand." Before she could answer, a well-dressed, middle aged couple sprang to their feet.

"Are you the young man who helped Abbey?" The tears that streamed down the woman's face as she looked wide-eyed at Nick, would be expected of a mother in this situation, but they looked strangely out of character for such a prim looking woman.

Before he could answer, the man, who looked just as prim as his wife, but much closer to fainting, said, "They told us that she would have died at the scene, had it not

TAMMY GACH

been for your quick and heroic actions! It's because of you that not only is our daughter alive, but they will most likely be able to save her hand!"

Cynthia Duggan clasped her husband's hand, and with tears in her eyes, she said, "My husband is right. You were there, and you jumped right in to help her. That is the best birthday present that she will ever get."

Nick was speechless. He nodded his head and choked back his tears as the couple hugged him, in what he assumed was an uncharacteristic display of emotion for them.

Nick knew. He could feel it in his gut, and the thought gave him goosebumps. This girl, was more than someone who he had helped. He did not just want to know the outcome. He felt *invested* in the outcome. Maybe it was just the intensity of the situation, but he did not think so. They were connected now - bonded in a way that he could not begin to understand - at least not yet.

"Abbey. Her name's Abbey." Her mother said. Nick smiled at both of her parents, and wiped the crocodile tears from his eyes.

OMINOUS WHISPERS

CHAPTER 37

"Mr. and Mrs. Duggan, Abbey's awake and doing well. You can come see her now if you'd like, before we move her up to her room." A bouncy, refreshed looking young man said.

Richard and Cynthia Duggan sprung to their feet before they were fully awake. They were relieved, and hardly noticed the pain that their bodies were suffering from dozing off upright in their chairs during the nine hour surgery. As they walked, hunched from back pain, they both turned around at the same time, to see Nick rubbing the sleep from his eyes.

TAMMY GACH

"She's awake, Nick!" Mr. Duggan said, as he pulled a starched handkerchief from his pants pocket, to cover his mouth while he cleared his dry throat.

"Is she gonna be OK, Doc?" Mr. Duggan turned to ask the young man.

"I'm not the doctor. I'm one of the post anesthesia care unit nurses, but the doctor is with her now, and I heard him tell her that the surgery went well, and that with rehab, she should get most of the function back."

"Oh, thank goodness! Do you want to see her, Nick?" Mrs. Duggan began to cry, then she pulled a pristine handkerchief, of her own, from her purse.

"You guys go." Nick said, waving them on. "I'll see her after she's all settled, if she's OK with having a visitor."

Richard and Cynthia Duggan gave Nick identical smiles of warmth and gratitude as they nodded to him, before following the nurse back to the recovery area.

A larger version of the kindly, elderly volunteer, was now seated behind the desk. Despite needing a cane, she got up and walked over to Nick, and put her hand gently on his forearm. "Miss Duggan is going to be moved up to her room on the fifth floor, soon. There's a lovely lounge up there. I will tell her parents, and her nurse that you will be waiting there, if you'd like?"

Nick was touched by her kindness. He noticed the thin, age-spotted skin of her hand on his arm, and the well-worn wedding ring that was permanently embedded in her ring finger. He could tell that those hands, gnarled with age, had soothed many over the years.

## CHAPTER 38

Blood was spraying everywhere – in his eyes, his nose, his mouth – he could not stop it. He became frantic as he tried harder and harder. She was going to die! *"Dammit! Do something! You're failing!"* He jumped and his heart gave a thud when he felt the hand shaking his shoulder.

"Nick! Calm down, son. We saw you in here when we walked by. You were twitching and talking in your sleep." It was Abbey's dad, trying to wake him as gently as he could. It took a moment for Nick to get his bearings. He looked around, and was surprised to see daylight coming through window of the fifth floor lounge. "Have you been here all night?" Mr. Duggan asked.

224

"Yeah, I guess I have." Nick stretched and tried not to blast Mr. Duggan with a shot of morning breath as he yawned.

"Abbey's awake, and the pain meds must be working because she's smiling and she's extra chatty this morning! We told her that you came to the hospital and waited with us. She says that she remembers you at the scene of the accident, but she thought that you were the Archangel Michael, and that the two of you were floating around in some big building, or house, or a church, or something."

Nick and Richard shared a chuckle of relief. "Angel or not, she's anxious to meet you. Don't tell her that I told you," Richard said with a grin, "But, when my wife told her what a handsome young man you are, Abbey drove the poor nurses nuts until they got her cleaned up!"

Nick asked a nurse for a patient sized toothbrush and tooth paste. He looked like he had slept on a chair all night, but at the very least, he did not want to stink. Fresh breathed, Nick walked into Abbey's room. He took one look at her, and his heart gave a thud nearly as big as the one he had when he was woken up from his nightmare. She was stunning. He had never seen hair quite that color before. It was not really what you could call blonde, or light brown, or even red. It was a striking golden color that was intensified by its silkiness. Despite all she had been through, she smiled when she saw him, and he could have sworn that he saw a twinkle come from her perfect teeth.

## CHAPTER 39

Nick looked across the table for two, and was captivated by the way that the flickering light from the candles seductively danced on the smooth, soft skin of his wife's face. He marveled at Abbey's recovery. It had been three years, and through her strength and determination, she had regained most of the function in her hand.

"Happy birthday, Mrs. Davis." Nick said, leaning forward on the table

"Happy birthday, Mr. Davis." Abbey replied, marveling at the love that radiated from his eyes every time that he smiled at her like that. That look made her swoon the first time that she saw it, and every time since then.

Nick reached across the table and gently pulled her hands to his face, and kissed them. "That day, three years ago..." Nick began.

Abbey nodded and looked down for a moment, glad that she did not remember much about that day.

"At the hospital, your mom mentioned that it was your birthday, but I was so happy to hear that you were going to be alright, that I totally forgot that it was mine and my brother's birthday too!"

"Yep." Abbey said with a smile. "I remember, you were visiting me, and it was – like what – three or four days later, when it dawned on you that we have the exact same birthday? When we learned that they were the same right down to the minute, we both just about fell out of our chairs!" Abbey chuckled. "Do you remember what I said to you when we realized that?"

"Yes I do!" Nick sat up straight, and wagged like a peacock. "You said, 'now we're going to have two things to celebrate on that day from now on.' But then I think that you thought that you may have sounded a little too forward, because you turned as red as these roses here on the table."

"Cute and perceptive." Abby said, playfully raising an eyebrow.

"Well, as it turned out, you weren't being forward at all, because I had already decided that I was going to marry you one day. And Look! I did!"

Nick leaned across the table to kiss his wife, dragging his necktie through the butter, forward and back.

"Cute, perceptive, and a complete slob!" He said, and they both laughed so loudly that the people at nearby tables turned to look.

TAMMY GACH

CHAPTER 40

On their way home from their birthday dinner, Abbey reached over, took Nick's hand, and put it on her thigh, under her skirt, just above her knee. Nick smiled, and more than eager to play along, he slowly ran his hand up her inner thigh. She watched for the expression on his face when he reached the top of her thigh-high stockings, and then nothing to get in the way of his fingers reaching the slippery warmth of her naked body.

His eyes widened, his ears became red, and his breathing became heavier. Just the reaction that she had

230

hoped for when she decided to wear thigh-highs and a garter belt, with no underwear.

"Oh boy." He said in a surprised whisper. "I'm gonna focus on driving, but I'll get right back to that, the second that we get home!" He said, reluctantly taking his hand from her crotch, and putting it back on the steering wheel. The sight and feel of Abby's severed hand, and all that blood, still haunted him, and he'd be damned if he was going to be the cause of her being in another accident.

Before Nick could get his sport coat all the way off, Abbey had him pinned against the bedroom wall, running her hands over every ripple of muscle beneath his white Brooks Brothers dress shirt. He reached between her legs and resumed rubbing, where he had left off. In no time, her body quivered and her muscles tightened as the first of three orgasms, that night, flooder her body with incomparable pleasure.

He stood up at the end of the bed, and slowly removed his clothes. In the beginning of their relationship, he felt ridiculous doing his mini strip tease, but now, he loved watching how turned on she got by seeing him undress. She loved his tall, broad shouldered swimmers build, and looked at it every chance she got. In Abbey's eyes, everything about Nick was perfection, from his short, wavy light brown hair, to his rock solid pecs, and all the way to his feet. She adored all of him, and she told anyone who would listen, that he is the most handsome man she had ever seen.

"Take off everything except those stockings and *connector units.*" He said. It still made them both laugh out loud whenever Nick called Abbey's garter belt a connector unit. He called it that the first time that she wore it for him, because he could not think of the name of the sexy piece of lingerie, but now they both called it that because it was an inside joke that they never grew tired of.

Nick and Abbey enjoyed every inch and depth of each other that night. Their passion and love for each other was so strong, that they were like two halves of an erotic, passion starved whole, that ached to come together. Abbey's hand had healed so well, that the touches from both of her hands felt the same when she touched his body. Whether she was seductively running them up the length of his thighs, or if she was raking them down his back during a moment of unconstrained passion, both of her hands were marvelously skilled.

CHAPTER 41

Naked, relaxed, and glistening with the sweat that came from their passion, Nick and Abbey clung to each other, staring at the full moon shining brightly through their bedroom window.

"You know that place that we've talked about that would make a great restaurant?" Abbey asked.

"You mean the old mansion, off of Shatsworth Road?" Nick asked. He turned his head toward Abbey, and could not help but be aroused by the way the moonlight bathed her naked silhouette.

"Umm hmm, that's the one. Well, my dad told me, when he called to wish us a happy birthday, that it's empty. With any luck, they'll put it on the market!"

Nick took a deep breath, and let it out slowly. "I know we've hoped for nearly the past three years that it would become available someday, but now that it might, I gotta say that it scares me a bit."

"Scares you in what way?" Abbey asked.

"In what way doesn't it scare me?" He said. "The expense, the renovations it'll need to be turned from an asylum to a restaurant, rumors about its creepy history, and most of all, I still don't get how we have both been obsessed with that place since way before we met. That's weird and a little creepy too."

"Yeah, I gotta say, that is pretty freaky-deaky, isn't it? But, it's a really cool old mansion, so I'll bet that a lot of people are drawn to it. And, if you think about it, its architectural charm, and its creepy history will probably mean lots of customers." Abbey said.

"So, the place isn't a looney bin anymore, huh?" Nick gave his wife an unsure, sideways glance.

"No." She said. "They closed that down a couple of years ago. I don't think that there were any dangerous

234

wackos there. From what I understand, it was more of a retreat for mentally stressed rich people. Hmm, anyway, did I ever tell you that when I was a teenager, my friends and I memorized the phone number of the asylum, and when a guy that we didn't want to go out with, would ask one of us for our phone number, then keep asking after we said no, we would give him the number to the asylum!" Abbey laughed, remembering how much fun she had as a teenager.

Nick scrunched his eyebrows and looked up at the ceiling for a moment, as if he were deep in thought. "You know, that happened to me once! I asked a pretty girl for her number, and she gave me the number to the looney bin. Woah! I wonder if that was you."

Abbey's jaw dropped a bit, and her eyes grew nearly as big as the moon that was shining on their bodies. "I...I...Uh." She stumbled over her words.

Nick broke into laughter. "I'm just teasing! No one ever gave me that phone number! Oh, I'm glad that moon is casting so much light in here, because I got to see the look on your face – I really got you!"

"Yes you did, you eeevil husband!" Abbey laughed and poked his ribs, the tickle fight did not take long to turn into round two of passion.

235

An hour later, too exhausted to move, they collapsed into each other's arms again. "You know what?" Abbey said. "Why don't we take a drive over there tomorrow and have a look around?"

"To the Knob Hill mansion?" Nick asked.

"Yeah. Why not?" She replied.

"Sure. I'll ask my brother to come, too. We both have a couple of days off, and besides, he's as obsessed with that place as we are!"

Nick fell asleep smiling that night, feeling like the luckiest guy in the world, to have such an amazing wife. He had a hard time believing the stories that she and her parents told, about how meek and afraid she was before the accident. He just could not picture the woman he loved, the woman who was so full of life, who loved adventure, ever being too afraid to follow her own path.

OMINOUS WHISPERS

CHAPTER 42

Nick had a playfully spirited evil grin on his face as he looked in his rear view mirror at his brother in the back seat, and at his wife in the passenger seat. "This is going to be interesting," he said as he pulled his SUV onto the circular driveway in front of Knob Hill mansion. He had hoped to elicit a reaction from one or both of them, knowing that they had mixed emotions about going there, but they were both too busy staring at the place. He had mixed emotions too. Seriously, it is pretty odd for three people to be so obsessed, intrigued and freaked out by a house that they have never been in. It was time to see if they could discover some reason why they felt so drawn to the mansion.

OMINOUS WHISPERS




CHAPTER 43




There was a white work van with a ladder strapped to the top, parked a little further up on the driveway, and the large mahogany front door of the mansion was wide open.

"Looks like someone's here, maybe doing a little spruce-up, or renovations." Abbey said as they got out of the SUV.

There was no one in sight, so Nick walked up to the open front door, knocked, and yelled out, "Hello! Anybody here?" No answer. After yelling a few more times, he looked at Abbey and Pete, shrugged his shoulders, and said, "Let's go in and look around."

"We can't just walk in!" Abbey said. "That's unlawful entry."

"Well, this was a looney bin you said. Right? I'm sure they must have had visitors, so we'll just say we thought it was still open if someone sees us and asks what we're doing here." Nick said.

"A mental health facility, is what I said." Abbey turned to Pete and said, "I suppose we could say that I'm checking out facilities for my delightfully unstable husband!" Pete chuckled, and Nick turned around to flash them the wackiest deranged face that he could make.

They got out of the SUV, stood on the gravel of the circular drive, and studied the mansion's façade and vast grounds, which spread across the only hill in an otherwise flat town.

"You know what this place reminds me of, Abbey?" Nick asked, as it dawned on him.

"No, Babe. What?" She replied without taking her gaze off the eerie beauty of the Tudor mansion's architectural style.

# OMINOUS WHISPERS

"It reminds me of that oil painting in your dad's study – you know, the one of the weathered, old sea captain. You look at his craggy, sun and sea battered face, expressionless, yet still brimming with a lifetime of wisdom, and no matter how hard you try, you simply can't imagine what he might have looked like as a child. It's almost as if he had to have been born looking just the same as he does in the painting. This place is the same way. I can't picture it being built, all those years ago, with new materials, and by human hands. To me, this place looks like it grew up from the earth and rock beneath it. Never new, and never different than it looks right now."

Abbey and Pete were staring at Nick. "Damn, Brother! I never knew your thoughts were so profound!" Pete joked.

"I know – right!" Abbey chimed in, but both she and Pete knew exactly what he was talking about, and agreed with him.

Nick wondered if that was the reason that he had been drawn to the place ever since the first time he saw it as a teen. When Nick and Pete were around fourteen or fifteen, they and a group of buddies, one of them was sixteen and had a new driver's license, drove out to Knob Hill one summer evening at dusk, because it was rumored to be a haunted psychiatric hospital. The boys each stole some of their father's beer from home, then headed off to see which of them could be scared the worst.

Nick and Pete were captivated by the mansion. Their apprehension grew as they walked closer, but then subsided after they sat against the brick retaining wall on the far side of the center statue, and downed a couple beers. Their buddy, Jimmy, puked his guts out on the grass, but that was more a result of mixing his dad's beer with his mom's wine, than it was from fear. Rick, the driver, told stories of electrical shock treatments, water torture, and forced castration of the severely insane residents of Knob Hill Asylum. Frank, a short kid, with dark hair, fair skin, and freckles, was the only boy who got totally freaked out, and begged to leave. Rick shined a flash light at him, and was about to tell him to stop being a puss, and drink another beer, when he noticed a wet spot on the front of Frank's pants, and busted out laughing.

"Frank pissed himself!" Rick howled.

"I did not! I spilled some beer!" Frank screamed, lunging at Rick, fed up with being bullied.

The other boys pulled Frank off of Rick, and shushed them both, for fear of a hospital worker seeing them. The last thing any of them wanted was the cops calling their parents to come and bail them out of jail for underage drinking and trespassing.

The twins had been out there many times since that night, but neither one could explain why. All they knew, was they were compelled to go and just look at the place. It was not until they were there, standing in front of the mansion when they were about twenty-one, when Pete looked at his brother and said, "This would make an awesome restaurant and bar, you know? Convert it, and make the entrance from the road more visible."

From then on, not only were they compelled to visit, but they were inspired as well. Today, however, was the first chance they ever had to go inside and look around.

## CHAPTER 44

Abbey entered the house behind Nick. The moment that she stepped inside, and took one look at the black and white marble floor, she stopped dead in her tracks. Pete, who was following closely behind her, did not expect her sudden stop. He ran into Abbey, stepping on her right heel and pulling off her shoe. Instant panic took her breath away, and Abbey practically climbed over Pete to get out of the mansion.

"What the hell happened?" Nick said as he followed his wife to see if she was OK.

Abbey leaned forward to catch her breath, and put her hand on her chest in reaction to her racing heartbeat. "It was just like my dreams about this place. You remember, they were really vivid when I was in the hospital after my accident?"

"Yeah," the twin brothers said in unison.

"This floor in the foyer – It was exactly the same in my dream. But that's not the freakiest part. My right leg and ankle were burning with pain in the dreams, just like when you stepped on it, Pete – only much worse!"

"Do you think that you were foreseeing us coming here?" Pete asked as he pulled a flask of whiskey out of the pocket of his cargo pants, and handed it to Abbey.

Abbey smiled at her brother-in-law. "Good idea!" She said, taking a big gulp of the whiskey, and then another. "I don't know, Pete. I always thought that the images in my mind were more like déjà vu, you know? More like this is somewhere that I have been, not somewhere that I was going."

After a third generous sized shot of whisky, Abbey had steeled herself enough to try going in again. With a death grip on both the guy's hands, Abbey did her best to ignore the pain that was worsening on the back of her leg, and through her rib cage. She was seeing the marble floor in

245

front of her as she walked along it, but she could also see it from above, in her mind's eye – and in that view, she was floating backwards.

Nick and Pete were not having any visions, or pains, but they were both feeling a building sense of anxiety – a vague need to do something, but they kept it to themselves, because they did not want to scare Abbey. Nick was becoming annoyed by the anxiety that he was feeling. He gently slipped the flask from Abbey's hand. He shook it a bit and was relieved to find that she had not polished off the entire thing. Nick was awestruck by the beauty of the mansion's interior, and he wanted to fully take in the grandeur of the place without the anxiety. The beautifully carved rich wood paneling, the arched plaster ceilings, and the scenes and characters from Chaucer's *The Canterbury Tales*, which were depicted in the massive stained glass windows, were captivating.

When they reached the end of the foyer, Abbey pointed down the hallway on their right, and said, "The kitchen is this way, second door on the left." Chills ran through their bodies as they stood and looked at each other. "How in the hell could I know that?" She said, in a voice that Nick recognized as the *she's about to cry* voice. But then, Abbey's demeanor changed in an instant. She furled her eyebrows and clenched her teeth so hard that her jaw muscles stood out, rigidly flexed. She turned, and in a determined gait, walked right in to that kitchen. Perplexed, the guys quickly followed.

Half way through the kitchen, Abbey stopped walking, and began looking. "Where is that fucking door?" She snarled as her eyes scanned the wall.

Nick and Pete were shocked. Abbey never cussed – not even while she was going through the painful and frustrating physical therapy sessions for her hand.

"There! There it is!" Abbey stepped forward a few feet, and pointed to a section of wall that was behind some empty stainless steel commercial shelves.

"Help me slide these shelves over." Abbey said.

Once the shelves were out of the way, she pushed on the wall. It sprung back toward her, just like she knew that it would, exposing the hidden staircase to the basement. Abbey turned, pushed past the guys, ran to the kitchen sink, and vomited.

Nick and Pete stood and stared at each other. For a moment, they were paralyzed by a blend of confusion and fear. They both could feel that ever-growing sense of dread, crawling up the back of their necks like a huge spider.

TAMMY GACH

In that moment, Nick considered saying, *the hell with it*, and they would leave and never look back. Then he realized, that was not an option. They were drawn to Knob Hill, whether they wanted to be or not. They may have wanted to be done with the mansion at that point, but it would soon become clear that the mansion was not done with them.

"Ok, guys. This is what we came here for. I think we kinda expected some weird shit, right?" Nick said as he rubbed Abbey's back and held her hair back from her face. "I know *I* did – I mean, think about it - we've all been drawn to this place our entire lives, right? But why? Pete, why did you and I start driving here to stare at this house every chance that we got, as soon as we were old enough to drive? And Abbey, how did you know that there was a hidden door in the kitchen, or even *where* the kitchen was?"

Abbey and Pete did not say a word, they just stood there and nodded. They knew that Nick was right. Abbey stepped toward the mysterious door to the basement, poked her head in and looked around. It was completely empty, except for the cob webs. She stepped on the top step with her right foot, and a burning pain shot through her calf, causing her to nearly fall down the stairs. Another image popped into her head. An image of this place, of these stairs. As she regained her footing, and continued down the stairs, she could see herself, in her mind's eye, going down them, scooting on her butt.

Nick and Pete started to follow Abbey. Nick was about to step down on the first step, when something pushed on his chest – hard – like a guy might get shoved by someone starting a fight. He fell back into the kitchen, taking his brother down with him. "Something just pushed me!" Nick squealed, in a voice that was so high pitched, that it surprised Pete and Abbey. "I mean, shit, something literally pushed me!"

They sat there, in confusion, just looking at each other for a moment, until Nick said, "Sorry, dude. I didn't mean to take you down with me."

An icy cold washed over Nick and Pete, leaving them as stunned as the time they fell through the thin ice of a creek that they were playing on as kids. Those words, *take you down with me,* hit them both with a déjà vu that chilled them to the core.

"Did you ever say that to me before?" Pete said, in slow hesitation.

"Yeah. I think I did." Nick said, just as slowly, and with just as much hesitation in his voice. Then, in unison, the twin brothers said, "At a window."

# TAMMY GACH

They jumped to their feet. "This is a deja-fucking-vu house!" Pete said, wrapping his arms around himself to try to warm the ice in his veins.

"No kidding!" Abbey said, vigorously nodding, only slightly relieved that she was not the only one experiencing the scary, baffling phenomena. She turned, and continued down the stairs. With each step, she was greeted with an increase in the level of pain that felt like arrows of fire shooting through her leg, rib cage, head and throat. A fog began to engulf her body, getting progressively darker and colder as she descended.

"Do you smell that?" She hollered to Nick and Pete, who were still in the kitchen, at the top of the stairs.

Push or no push, Nick wasn't about to let his wife be in that creepy-ass basement all by herself. The basement was ready to let him in. He was expecting to be pushed back again, but the resistance never came. Pete followed. They sniffed the air as they came down to the basement.

"Other than the musty basement smell, it smells like gunpowder – you know – like a gun's just been fired." Nick said, looking around the bitterly cold basement, brows furled. His instinct to protect Abbey, and his curiosity, overruled his trepidation.

# OMINOUS WHISPERS

"I don't smell it." Pete said, sniffing deeper as he made his way to Nick and Abbey. "I probably can't smell it because it's so damn cold down here that my nose is ready to crack off of my face!"

Without a word, Nick turned his wide-eyed face, pale with fear, toward his brother, and pointed at the basement window on the far wall.

"Holy shit!" Pete said. His heart began to race, and he could feel it kick and skip some beats. The oppressive darkness of tunnel vision was surrounding him. He took a deep breath, and bent forward with his hands on his knees. He hoped that it would be enough to keep himself from passing out. "That's the window we were looking in when you said that thing about not wanting to take me out with you. Isn't it?"

"Yeah. It is." Nick replied.

"Yeah." Abbey said, as huge tears welled up in her eyes. "I remember you coming through that window. I'm remembering it all. It's all coming to me. Oh my God! Oh my God, you guys died trying to rescue me!"

The memories came flooding back to all three, like a tidal wave of the images, emotions and sensations that, when put together, illustrated their lives – their past lives, the lives that were cut way too short.

251

The three of them huddled together, and pulled each other close in a bear hug – afraid to let go, but also afraid to stay.

"I was going to tell you, that day, after work, that I decided to go to Michigan State, but I never got the chance." Abbey said, looking at Nick, while the tears rolled down her cheeks.

Nick smiled. He held his wife's face in his hands, and looked in her eyes with a passion that told her that he knew exactly what she was talking about.

"Hey, guys." Pete said, taking a step back and looking around. "The cold! It's gone! It's warming up in here!"

"It is!" Abbey said, as she held out her arms. "My pain is gone all of a sudden too!"

"I was getting one mother-of-a-headache, but that's gone now too!" Nick said.

For a moment, the three of them looked around, and looked at each other, for some bizarre, yet logical answer. Each of them wondered silently if they were dreaming.

"Let's go." Abbey said. "I think we've seen more than enough for one day."

## OMINOUS WHISPERS

The guys nodded, and as they walked up the hidden staircase, and made their way out of Knob Hill, all three of them knew that it was not a dream. It simply was what it was.

# CHAPTER 45

Dead silence, like the vacuum of outer space, filled the SUV as they drove home. Nick glanced at Abbey, and saw that she had goose bumps and was shivering. He looked at his dashboard and saw that the temperature inside the vehicle was 80 degrees. In his shocked state of mind, Nick had not thought to turn the air conditioning on.

"Are you cold, Hun?" Nick said as he rubbed the top of her leg.

The broken silence, and Nick's touch, made Abbey jump. "Uh, no. I'm still freaked out by what just happened." She rubbed her arms, noticing the shivers and goose bumps. "Hey, Pete." She turned and looked at her wide-eyed, stunned brother-in-law, in the back seat. "Do you have anything left in that flask? I need to knock my anxiety level down a few dozen notches or so!"

Pete managed a half smile. "No, and if I did, it woulda been gone ten seconds after we got back in the car!"

"I'll tell you what, guys. I'll stop at a party store and pick up some beer and tequila. We'll go back to our place, drown our jitters, and try to figure out why this happened to us."

Pete and Abbey nodded.

# CHAPTER 46

The last time that Pete needed a drink this badly, was the day three years earlier, when he had to pack Abbey's severed hand in ice. Nick and Pete went to the kitchen, got three shot glasses from the cupboard, opened the tequila, and threw the beer in the freezer for a quick chill. Nick grabbed a lime from the crisper drawer of the fridge, and cut it into wedges.

"Weirded out or not, there's no reason to not enjoy a good tequila the proper way!" Nick said, as he looked toward the living room, relieved that his wife did not see him forget to use the cutting board.

# OMINOUS WHISPERS

"Very true, brother. Very true."

Nick carried a tray with the tequila, shot glasses and wine to the spacious living room, and set it on the ottoman near the fireplace, between the two toile upholstered sofas. Abbey opened the Victorian walnut armoire that hid the flat screen TV. She connected her laptop computer to the television, so that the three of them would not have to sit in a cluster to see the screen.

Nick poured three shots of tequila, and raised his in the air. "Here's to…" He hesitated, not knowing what to say to toast this very unusual drinking occasion.

"How about, here's to drinking enough to stop the trembling." Pete said, tequila sloshing over the brim of his shot glass, because he truly was still shaking.

"Hey, that's alcohol abuse!" Abbey joked about the spilled alcohol, as a way to lighten the mood. Then she said, "OK, I think I'll start by typing the name of the property into the search engine, and see what comes up." The guys nodded, eyes glued to the large screen of the TV.

The hit that caught every one's attention was a newspaper article from Monday, August 28, 1978, titled: *The Tragic History of the Knob Hill Mansion.* Abbey clicked on it, and they all began to read the article to themselves.

# TAMMY GACH

*The three teens, and two adults, who were murdered at the Shatsworth/Willis historic Knob Hill Mansion this past Thursday, were not the first to die at the ominous Tudor style estate. According to historical and Shatsworth family records, the first person to die at the property was Ansley Shatsworth, the youngest son of Simon Shatsworth, Sr.*

*Less than one week after construction was completed on the nineteen room mansion, Ansley Shatsworth, age twenty-one, was found bludgeoned to death in his bedroom. Although never substantiated, it was rumored that the younger Shatsworth son was having an affair with the wife of his older brother, Simon Junior. No one was ever indicted for the crime, and neither the murder, nor the alleged affair garnered much attention from the press, at the time, in deference to the Shatsworth family's request for privacy.*

*Another death at the mansion, deemed to be a suicide, occurred in 1937, when Ilse Shatsworth jumped to her death from the roof of the mansion.*

"Holy crap!" Pete said. The three of them looked at each other, stunned and bewildered.

Abbey gasped. "Holy crap is right! Did you happen to notice that the day and year that the teens were murdered, the Thursday before the date the article was published, is the same day *and* year that all three of us were born?"

The hair stood up on the back of Nick's neck, giving him that *"someone just stepped on my grave"* type of chill through his body. He looked at the article more closely. "Oh my God! It is!" He said. "So, is it a creepy coincidence, or did the souls of those murdered teenagers enter our bodies because we were being born while they were dying, or is the place haunted by those murdered kids, and they're somehow sending us messages? I don't know what the hell to think!"

Abbey rubbed the goosebumps from her arms, and took another shot of tequila. "There's no way that it can be a coincidence. If it was just the birth and death dates, then sure, I would say coincidence. But not when you combine it with what happened to us while we were there, and how we've all been drawn to that place. We're them reincarnated. As crazy as that sounds, it's the most logical thing that I can think of."

Nick stood up, and put both of his hands on his head, hoping to rub the pounding fear from his skull. Saying nothing, he went to the kitchen, took the six-pack of beer from the freezer, and brought it to the living room. They each opened a beer, and poured another shot.

Pete loudly released a deep breath of air through his nose, as he clapped his hands down on his thighs. "It is kinda out there, but it makes sense. I mean, it would explain why the place seemed to want us to leave, and the déjà vu that we all got, and like you said, Abbey, our lifelong obsession with it."

The booze was kicking in hard, but they were able to find two more articles about the Knob Hill mansion. One of the articles, from November, 1979, read: *Thomas Willis, 21 and Heir to the Shatsworth-Willis Fortune, Found Guilty of Bank Robbery, Kidnapping, and the Murder of His Parents and Three Teens at Knob Hill Mansion. Willis Sentenced to Life at the State Hospital for the Criminally Insane.* The other article read: *Knob Hill Estate to be leased to Wayne Hospital, for New Psychiatric Rehabilitation Rest Home.*

Trepidation turned to bravado, and focus turned to fog. Abbey closed her laptop with a resolute slam. Slurring her words, she said; "I think I've had enough of this…reading about this murder and crazy crap." Suddenly, sadness replaced the drunken haze that filled her mind. "I can't imagine how our parents…uh, their parents, or whoever, must have felt when they found out that their kids were murdered."

# OMINOUS WHISPERS

The guys were quiet for a moment. Memories of Walt, Diane, and Karen Greer brought a happy warmth to Nick's heart, until he thought about the pain that they must have endured, following Ted's death. "I've had enough of it too." Nick said. "Let's order a pizza to soak up some of this booze that we drank."

"Yeah, and you stay here tonight Pete...You...You're in no shape to drive!" Abbey said just before her head hit the pillow on the couch.

Pete wasn't sure whether to laugh or cry. "Well, that was one way – not the best way – but it was one way for Billy to get the hell away from the shit stains that he had for parents." He said.

## CHAPTER 47

"What the hell!  Did a truck hit me last night?"  Nick said, as he got out of bed and staggered to the bathroom to pee, brush the funk from his teeth and tongue, and down some aspirin.

"Ooohhh!  Hangover food.  I need hang over food, husband!"  Abbey replied, afraid to lift her head from the pillow.

When they got downstairs, Pete was already awake, but in no shape to do much more than sit with his head in his hands.  He peered, slit-eyed, from the gap between his fingers. The half-empty pizza box, beer cans and empty booze bottle reminded him of why he felt like a lump of dog poo this morning.

"Hangover food. Heavy, greasy hangover food." He mumbled.

"Yep. That's already been decided." Abbey said, handing him the bottle of aspirin.

TAMMY GACH

CHAPTER 48

"Aargh! I'm still hungover from last night." Abbey said, later that day, as she raised her sunglasses just enough to look at her puffy, bloodshot eyes in the mirror of the passenger side visor.

"I'm right there with ya, woman." Nick said in a tired, raspy voice. "Why didn't we just cancel dinner with your parents?"

Abbey sighed, slightly annoyed that he even had to ask. "You know as well as I do, that my parents think that it's sweet that you and I were born on the same day, at the same time, at the same hospital, separated only by a wall between the two delivery rooms. So, they're going to continue to make a big deal about our birthday, and I know that you don't want to disappoint them any more than I do. They put a lot of work into our birthday dinner every year."

"I know. You're right. At least they don't schedule it on our actual birthday. They let us have that day to ourselves." Nick said. He paused, and thought of something funny. "What if Pete would have been the second one out of the chute? Then I would be the twin who was born two minutes before you guys. Does that mean that you would have married him instead of me?"

Abbey smiled. "Yes Nick. That's exactly what would have happened."

They smiled at each other, and held hands − both of them amused by his silly question, and her witty sarcasm.

The sight of her childhood home filled Abbey with a warm, safe feeling of familiarity every time that she visited. The stately white brick Georgian mansion, with its deep red front door, and the beautiful cloud-like cherry blossoms that bloomed each spring on the Yoshino tree in the front yard, tugged at her heart strings, as if to say *welcome home*. Not only did her childhood home, and her parents welcome her, but Scout, the ancient Springer

Spaniel who lived next door, had been greeting Abbey with a single *"come pet me"* bark, for as long as she could remember. Scout's cordial bark was becoming softer, and more tired, as the years went by. Even though he no longer stood on his hind legs with his front paws on the fence, for ease of petting access, he still enjoyed love and attention from the neighbors, just as much as he always had.

"I know that we'll talk about Knob Hill with your parents, but I don't think that we should mention our *"Twilight Zone experience"* to them." Nick said, as they walked from the car to greet Scout, before going inside.

"Oh, I totally agree. They would either laugh, or have us committed. Either way, it wouldn't be good!" Abbey said, and then she paused for a moment, not sure if what she had to say next, would make Nick think that she was crazy. "Speaking of Knob Hill, ever since I woke up this morning, I've had this gnawing desire in the back of my mind, to go back."

"I know exactly what you mean! I've been fixated on it all day. It's like the way I've always been drawn to it, except now it's a lot stronger

OMINOUS WHISPERS

CHAPTER 49

"The lamb chops are pure heaven, Mom!"

"Um hmm!" Nick nodded in agreement, his mouth stuffed with his mother-in-law's wonderful cooking.

"Thank you. I'm delighted that you are enjoying them!" Cynthia said, displaying only a soft smile to indicate that she was beaming with pride. Only a well-bred, gentlewoman, such as Cynthia Duggan could convey so much with such understated and refined mannerisms.

"Cooked to perfection, Cynthia! I am a lucky man!" Richard said to his wife, with a smile of adoration. "So, tell us – what have you two been up to lately?" He asked, genuinely interested.

Nick and Abbey looked at each other, both thinking *here we go!* Nick paused, like he always did, when he and Abbey were both asked a question. He learned, the hard way, that the lady should be allowed to speak first, when it was loudly pointed out to him, one time, at a cocktail party, by Abbey's mostly deaf grandfather.

"Nick, Pete and I took a little drive over to Knob Hill yesterday. We were intrigued after you had mentioned that it may be coming on the market soon." Abbey told her father.

"Oh, is that so?" Richard sat a little straighter in his chair and smiled. He was clearly pleased with the topic of conversation. "Are you still considering it as a location for a restaurant, Nick?"

"Yes, Sir. I think we are."

"You are, or you *think* you are?"

Richard was a lawyer through to his core. He chose his words carefully, and expected precise answers to his questions. To those who did not know him, he could be seen as snooty or condescending, but nothing could be further from the truth. He cared about people, and he understood that the fate of his client's futures rested squarely on his shoulders. He also understood that his precision won cases.

# OMINOUS WHISPERS

"Well, Dad." Abbey took the linen napkin from her lap, and dabbed her mouth. "We're a bit concerned about the history of the place."

"I can appreciate that. It does have a bit of dark history, doesn't it?" Richard nodded.

"I would say, more than a *bit* of dark history, Dear." Cynthia added.

"Quite true, my love. Quite true." He nodded again, in acknowledgement. "Here are some things to consider," he said, making eye contact to politely include everyone. "Yes, people did die in the house. Gruesome deaths, to be sure. The macabre backdrop, however, will likely be an advantage, as well. Murder houses, as I've heard them called, typically stay on the market for a long time, and in the end, sell for far less that the asking price. Most people don't want to live in a house where horrific things have happened, but someone will end up buying it simply because the lure of a good deal is stronger than their fear. Another thing, you won't be living there, or sleeping there. It will be your business, not your home, even though it's zoned for business or residential. The last thing to consider, is that people love spooky things. I think that the mansion's dark history will be almost as big of a draw as your and your brother's cooking, Nick!"

"Well, thank you for saying so, Sir! As I'm sure you know, not only is your daughter beautiful, but she's brilliant as well!" Nick smiled and reached across the table to touch his wife's hand. "She pointed out the very same thing to me, the other day. Like you, Sir, she also believes that the history will draw people to the restaurant and the up-scale bar. As a matter of fact, Abbey's been much less hesitant than I have been."

Cynthia and Richard smiled. "I am so proud of you, both!" Cynthia said, as a tear came to her eye. "Abbey, you have come so far in the past few years. You have really come into your own, and you are finally taking the world by storm!"

A rush of pride and a sense of accomplishment, like nothing she had ever felt before, washed over Abbey when she heard her mother say those words – *Taking the world by storm*. Without warning, tears streamed down Abbey's cheeks.

"Are you OK, Hun?" Nick asked her, confused by the magnitude of her reaction.

Oh, yes…yes, I'm fine. Just a really weird déjà vu feeling hit me. Abbey shook it off, and wiped the tears from her face.

# OMINOUS WHISPERS

*Maybe buying the mansion isn't such a great idea.*
Nick thought. More instances of creepy déjà vu was the
last thing that he wanted for Abbey, or for himself. Worse
yet, he believed that the mansion had the ability to
physically hurt them, or even drive them insane if it
wanted to. Nick would never forgive himself if something
happen to Abbey. He wished that he could tell her parents
exactly what had happened to them at the mansion, just to
get an outside perspective, but he knew that he could not.
Abbey's parents had to remain clueless about the strange
things that they had experienced over the past couple of
days.

The sound of Cynthia's voice, eloquent and cultured,
guided Nick's worried mind back to the conversation.
"How does that saying go, dear?" She asked.

In unison, Abbey and her father recited, "Learn from
the turtle – You can't move forward without sticking your
neck out a little!"

"Nick, I really do believe that you are our Abbey's
guardian angel. It wasn't that horrific accident that gave
her the confidence and fearless drive that she has now. It
was you – being there – then and now. She was always
capable of it, but she just wouldn't unleash it until you
came into her life." Richard said, raising his wine glass
for a toast.

271

"Dad's right. You saved me in more ways than one, that day. I realized that I needed to live my life. The full, adventurous life that I think I was destined to live, not the life of a little mouse, trembling in the corner, certain that there's nothing waiting for me out there other than a hungry cat. My love for you, not only for saving me and my hand, but for the man that you are, drives me to strive harder each and every day to be the kind of wife that lifts you up, and struggles with you, right by your side as you build your dream. I guess, I just want to make you the happiest that I can possibly make you."

Nick was the one with the tears in his eyes after Abbey said that. "I find it hard to believe that you were ever like a timid mouse." He said, wiping his eyes.

"It's true." Abbey said with a sigh. "I never wanted to follow in my parents footsteps and become a lawyer, but it was the safe thing to do. I would have a job, and mentors, and I knew that their reputation would help smooth my road through law school. I always needed a safety net. I used to always sweat the small stuff – you know – worry about every little thing. That reminds me, I recently saw a man on TV, whose young daughter was abducted and killed. He was a successful businessman, and he said that before his daughter was killed, he would sweat the small stuff, to the point of having stomach ulcers. He said he was too busy doing that to think of the really big, really bad things that can come along and derail one's life – that is, until the one big bad thing that he never even considered, did happen. He lost everything – his daughter, his wife, his house – it all fell apart after that. He said that he believes that if he would have been more focused on the things that mattered most, and lived his life to its fullest every day, it might not have saved his daughters life, but he at least would have spent more time enjoying being with her rather than tending to minutia."

"Love of family, and living one's life to the fullest, I believe, are the keys to the kingdom!" Richard said with a smile. "Not only that, but they are also two of the reasons that, if you'll allow me, I would love to invest in your future, and give you the money to buy Knob Hill."

The magnitude of the gesture left Nick and Abbey in stunned silence for a moment.

"Really, Dad? I don't know what to say!"

"How about, yes, and I love you Dad!" Richard said to Abbey.

"Yes! I love you, Dad! And you too, Mom!" Abbey jumped from her chair and hugged her parents. She looked at Nick, and saw concern in his eyes, rather than the elation that she expected. "Well, I mean, of course Nick and I will need to discuss it."

# TAMMY GACH

"Are you sure that the mansion doesn't scare you? I mean with all the murders and weird things that have happened there, Abbey." Nick asked.

"I think it's a house. A really big house in which a lot of bad things happened. But I don't think that a house has a soul, at least not in the same sense that people have souls. I think that the essence of a house, or the feel that a certain house can give you, you know, like homey, or creepy, or whatever, is put on that house by the people who live there. So I think that we would be the perfect people to give that place another chance by filling it with happiness and love."

Nick knew exactly what his wife was getting at when she said, *I think that we would be the perfect people to give that place another chance.* She meant that the mansion could shake off some of its creepy essence, by giving Ted, Billy, and Sandy another chance. He knew she was thinking that, because he woke up that morning with the same thought.

"So, do you think that's the reason that all three of us have been mesmerized by that mansion? That it's drawing us there to give it a second chance?"

"Yep. That's exactly what I think." Abbey said, straightening her posture, like she learned in law school, to portray an air of confidence.

274

# OMINOUS WHISPERS

The mansion was getting through to them. Calming their fears by the minute, drawing them back.

"Well, I don't understand all that *New Age* stuff, but I do know a gold mine when I see one." Richard said.

Nick looked around the table at three of the best people in his life, all smiling at him, filled with love and encouragement. "What the hell...oops! I'm sorry. I mean, what the heck. Why not. If they'll sell it, we'll buy it!" He said. "But, are you sure about the money, Sir?"

"I am quite sure, Nick. I know that the three of you have quite a bit of money saved to go toward opening a restaurant, but believe me, you'll need all of it to pay for renovations and equipment. Oh, and one more thing. I think it's about time that you start calling us *Mom and Dad*, instead of Sir and Ma'am." Richard said with a smile.

*They understand, Tom. They understand that they were chosen.* The sweet soft whispers in Tom's ear, continued on through the night, singing and lulling him into a peaceful sleep.

## CHAPTER 50

"Hey Honey, I found it!" Abbey called out to Nick.

"Wow! That was quick!" Nick said, holding his hand over his mouth to prevent the huge bite of turkey sandwich from falling out.

"Are you eating again? We just finished breakfast!" Abbey Said.

"Yeah." Nick said, ignoring her gaze of disbelief. "I'm surprised that you're not hungry, since you barely touched your breakfast."

"I guess I'm still not feeling well after drinking so much the other day. Anyway, I just went to the county Register of Deeds online." Abbey took a closer look at the computer screen. A cold chill ran up her spine. She had another of the all-too-frequent déjà vu flashes when she saw the name on the recorded deed. "Jeffrey Bane. Does that name mean anything to you, Nick?"

"Yeah, somehow, but I'm not sure how. It's weird. Now that I'm having memories of these past life experiences, some of the memories just aren't as clear as others."

"I know! I'm having the same thing. Some are just a quick flash, then they're gone." Abbey turned back to the computer screen. "No phone number for Mr. Bane, but I can probably get it from the law office data base. I guess law school wasn't a total waste of time after all." Abbey laughed.

"Well, not too much longer, and you can quit practicing law all together. You'll be too busy decorating and getting our restaurant up and running!"

Abbey loved that Nick always seemed to know the right thing to say to cheer her up.

"Will Pete be OK with me calling Mr. Bane to see if he's interested in selling?  After all, we're all equal partners in this." Abbey said.

"He'll be more than OK with it.  I told him what you said about houses, and souls, and second chances, and he told me that he came to the same conclusion.  So now, he's a lot less freaked out, and a lot more excited about getting it going.  He even did a little dance when I told him about your dad's offer." Nick laughed.

"OK, Babe.  Time to get to work.  Call me from the office if you get ahold of Bane."

"Will do." Abbey said, kissing Nick while she slipped her foot into her shoe.

OMINOUS WHISPERS

CHAPTER 51

"Hello, am I speaking with Mr. Jeffrey Bane?" Abbey asked, hoping that her nervous excitement was not obvious in her voice.

"Yes, I'm Jeff Bane."

"Hi, Mr. Bane. My name is Abbey Davis. The reason for my call is that I understand that you own the property known as Knob Hill...."

He interrupted, "Look Ms. Davis, I'm not interested in having any of those paranormal, ghost hunter TV shows filming the place."

"Oh, no. I think I may have given you the wrong impression, Mr. Bane. I'm not with a TV show, and I'm definitely not a ghost hunter. I just wanted to ask if you might consider selling. My husband and I love the house and the property, and we would like to buy it – that is, if the price is fair."

Jeff paused for a moment. "Do you have any idea of the horrific things that happened in that mansion over the years? I can't imagine anyone in their right mind wanting to live there. Hell, even the crazies that the hospital kept out there didn't stay!" He said, only half joking.

"Yes, Mr. Bane. We've done some research on the tragic history of Knob Hill, so yes, we're aware."

"Well, you kinda caught me out of the blue. I wasn't expecting this. Other than paying the maintenance company every month for upkeep, and paying the taxes, I try not to think about that place at all. I'll tell you what, you give me your phone number, and I'll talk it over with my brother to see what he thinks."

"Your brother?" Abbey asked.

"Uh-huh, my half-brother Tom. If you did any amount of research on the place, I'm sure you came across the name Tom Willis."

# OMINOUS WHISPERS

"Yes, Mr. Bane. I did read about the incident involving your brother."

"I have the final decision, of course, because he signed it over to me before his trial. His lawyer said if the property stayed in his name, and he was found criminally insane, it would be much harder for him to do anything with it, except maybe lose it to the state." Jeff let out a long, troubled sigh. "For some bizarre reason, after everything that happened out there, he still loves that place." Jeff knew that he had given Abbey more information than necessary. He wanted to gauge her reaction, because who in their right mind would want to buy Knob Hill, if they really knew what happened there? *Strange.* He thought.

"I'm a lawyer myself, so I know how these thing can go. And I must say Mr. Bane, it's very thoughtful of you to consider your brother."

After the phone call, Jeff could not get the sound of Abbey's voice out of his head. There was just something so familiar and comforting in that voice.

TAMMY GACH

CHAPTER 52

*I need to get a hobby, other than pouring my first scotch of the day, before noon.* Jeff said to himself, shaking his head as he poured this one at 10:00 a.m. But, he condoned today's early start, because he was not sure that he wanted to talk to Tom about selling the mansion, and because a good single-malt scotch always helped him think more clearly – or so he told himself.

The drink went down quickly, and the decision came instantly – He had to tell Tom that someone wanted to buy the place, even if it *did* upset him. People had lied to Tom and used him his entire life – that is of course, up until that day in 1978 when he put an end to it. Jeff never did lie to his brother. He loved him, and he still ached with the guilt of Tom being locked up, while he walked free. The district attorney had believed that Tom was covering for his brother, but still refused to indict him. Even with Jeff's confession, he did not believe that there was enough physical evidence to convict him.

Jeff looked around at the familiar décor of the only house that he had ever lived in. He sighed, and hung his head. There was so much to feel guilty about. He killed the only man that his mother had ever loved. He watched her cry herself to sleep every night, for five years following Alfred's death, until she died of a heart attack. At twenty-one years old, Jeff inherited the house that Alfred bought for his mother, and the two million dollars in trust funds that Alfred had set up for his illegitimate son. Now, nearly thirty years later, his once raven black hair, completely gray, and his leathery face, chiseled with age lines, added a good ten years to his actual age of fifty, Jeff still believed that his mother died from a broken heart – because of him.

Tears welling in his eyes, Jeff grabbed his keys and headed out to Wayne Hospital for the Criminally Insane, to see Tom.

# CHAPTER 53

"Hey Bro!" Jeff said with a smile and a wave as the nurse led him into the cafeteria where Tom was patiently waiting for lunch time to begin. He liked to be at least an hour early for every meal so he could pick a table as far away from the more violent patients as he could get.

"Jeff! Good to see you!" Tom said, standing to give his brother a handshake. The brothers quit hugging as a greeting, years earlier, after one of the patients teased Tom because he was *a boy hugging a boy.*

"Aren't you gonna ask why I'm here on a Tuesday, when I always visit on Fridays?" Jeff asked, sitting down at the table across from Tom.

"Nope, because I think I know why."

"OK, tell me what you think, and we'll see if you're right." Jeff smiled. Even after thirty years, Jeff was often surprised by some of the intuitive, if not downright prophetic, things that Tom would say – and this time was no different.

"Because of the phone call that you got from Sandy this morning."

The shock hit Jeff like a medicine ball to the chest. He had not heard the name Sandy since Tom's bench trial back in the late seventies. "Sandy? I got a call from a woman named Abbey Davis." Jeff said, eyes scrunched in curious anticipation of what Tom might say next.

"Yep, that's her. She wants to buy Knob Hill."

Jeff's jaw dropped. "Yeah, she does. But, how do you know that, and why did you call her Sandy?" Jeff's voice cracked as he said her name.

"The mansion told me – oh, and Jeff – how sweet it sounded this time – the soft whisper, and I could even feel the smooth scrolls of the woodwork on my fingertips as it whispered." Tom said wistfully, as if he was in the piano room at that moment, and not in a psych prison. Tom snapped back from his moment of longing, and looked at

285

Jeff. "I called her Sandy, because that's who she is. Why else would she want to buy the place? I'll tell you why. Because she needs to. It's time."

Tom had said a lot of bizarre things over the years, but this really had Jeff freaked out. He tried to put on a poker face, but then he thought back to the phone call. Abbey's voice... "Oh my God!" Jeff said. "That was Sandy's voice on the phone! Oh, God – that's why she sounded so familiar!" The blood drained from Jeff's face, and he grabbed tight to the sides of his chair to steady his trembling hands. "How? How can this be? How can she be Sandy?"

"It's all souls, Jeff. New souls, old souls. It's what makes us who we are – the soul. Some just don't get a fair shake, and some have a lot of lives to pass through before the finally figure out what they need to know. And, shit – some just get it right the first time around!" Tom said with a chuckle.

"How do you know all of this stuff? I mean, you have such insight. You know, Tom, that you're not crazy like they say you are, keeping you here, locked up with a bunch of loons! They don't understand you! Hell, I don't understand a lot of the things that you say, but one thing's for sure – I sure as hell believe you!" Jeff said, leaning across the table and lowering his voice, wanting to keep out of ear shot of the burly nurse with the itchy, Haloperidol trigger finger.

"I don't know, really." Tom said. "All I know is the mansion has been whispering to me for as long as I can remember."

"So, you want me to sell it to Sandy…or Abbey…or whoever you want me to call her?" Jeff asked.

"Well, I think you should. Actually, I think that you kinda have to." Tom said. Then he added, "Can you bring her here to visit me? Her…and the other two." He asked, with a childlike innocence.

"The other two?"

"Yeah. It's time for all three of them to get another chance. I killed those boys that night. I could hear the mansion, but I ignored it, and I brought evil to Knob Hill, just like everyone before me had done. And, you know what, Jeff?"

Jeff shook his head – no.

"The three who want to buy Knob Hill – Abbey, her husband, and her brother-in-law – they were chosen. They were drawn to the mansion because they have love in their hearts. The mansion needs that."

287

Jeff did not entirely understand what Tom was saying, but Tom understood. That was good enough for Jeff. "OK, Bro. All I can do is ask them. You know, some people don't like to come to places like this, but I'll definitely ask."

Tom looked around, sniffed deeply, and then smiled. "Lunch is just about ready!"

Jeff stood up and patted his brother on the back. "I'll leave you to it then." He smiled for Tom's benefit, but the second that he was out of view, sadness filled his eyes. Jeff hated the thought that Tom's early life had been so horrific, that living in a psychiatric hospital, full of violent criminals, wailing at night, and flinging their feces at the nurses during the day, was a big step up in his living condition.

OMINOUS WHISPERS

CHAPTER 54

"Are you sure that you want to do this?" Nick asked
Abbey as they drove down I-94 toward the state
psychiatric hospital. He already knew that Pete did not
want to – The nervous bouncing of his leg against the back
of Nick's seat, said it all. "I don't know about you, but I'm
as scared as hell to go and mingle amongst a bunch of
violent psychopaths!" Nick said.

"Glad I'm not the only one freaking out about this!"
Pete chimed in.

"Yeah, I'm sure." Abbey said. "I'm really not nearly as afraid, as I am curious."

Nick glanced at Abbey. He expected to see some outward sign that she was afraid, and that she was just putting on a brave face, for his sake. But, no. She looked as happy and relaxed as if they were heading out on vacation. He was perplexed. He did not know if he should be proud of his wife's bravery, or worried that she might be going insane.

"You guys don't have to go in if you don't want to. You can wait in the car."

For a moment, Nick thought that his wife might be teasing him, or angry with him for being afraid, but the look on her face told him that she was simply concerned about him. "No way!" He said. "I wouldn't let you go into that place by yourself! Scared or not, I'm going in, if you're going in!"

*Dammit!* Pete thought. *If Nick's going in, I guess I'll have to go in.*

"I won't be alone." Abbey said. "Jeff's going to meet us outside the main entrance, remember?" Abbey realized that she might have sounded as if she were ungrateful that Nick worried about her safety, so she continued. "I love how much you love, and want to protect me." She smiled.

# OMINOUS WHISPERS

"I'm glad that you're going to go in. I do feel safer when you're with me."

Nick smiled and squeezed Abbey's hand. He knew that she said that to keep his ego from being bruised. She had a way of building him up and making him feel valued. It was one of the many reasons why he cherished her, and would not hesitate to dive into the bowels of hell, if it would keep her safe.

"You two love birds realize that, if we really are right about being reincarnated, this guy who we're visiting, killed us thirty something years ago. You do realize that – right?"

They rode the rest of the way there, in bone-chilling silence.

# CHAPTER 55

Jeff smiled and offered his hand as Nick, Pete and Abbey approached. "Thank you for being willing to do this. Not many people would be willing to go to a psych hospital to meet someone that they don't know."

Both Nick and Abbey said, "Oh, no problem!" Pete just smiled cordially.

A tall, burly guard met them at the door, and checked their driver licenses. Pete felt some relief when he saw how formidable the guard looked. His skin was such a dark black, that it was almost indistinguishable from the dark navy blue of his uniform. *Even the craziest of dudes wouldn't mess with a guy like that*. Pete thought.

They passed through the metal detectors, and each were given a clip-on badge that read: "Visitor." A young, petite woman greeted them in the waiting room. She was dressed in business professional clothing, except for the running sneakers with orange laces. A piece of black electrical tape covered the name on her badge, but not the title "RN". The perceptive young nurse noticed that Nick and Abbey were looking at the badge and the peculiar choice of shoes.

"People always wonder." She said with a warm smile. "Most of us cover our name. The last thing that I want is for a released patient to look me up online to get my home address. And the gym shoes – well, you never know, in this place, when you might need to run."

Every bit of worry that Pete had prior to seeing the hulking guard, came rushing back.

"This place is huge!" Nick said, as the tiny nurse lead them down one hallway, then another, on the way to the visiting room. His wide eyes darted to and fro, looking and hoping that the guard had an equally massive twin brother stationed at this end of the hospital.

# TAMMY GACH

"Tom," Jeff said as they entered the visiting room. "This is Mrs. Davis, Mr. Nick Davis, and Mr. Peter Davis. The folks who are interested in buying Knob Hill."

"I'm very happy that you came to visit with me for a while." Tom stood and put out his hand to Abbey first. She was surprised by the gentleness of his huge hand.

"Thank you." Tom said as he shook the brother's hands.

"No problem. And please, call us Nick, Abbey and Pete." Nick said, hoping that his forced smile appeared genuine. In his terrified mind, Nick pictured Tom picking him up, and throwing him across the room like a rag doll.

Tom extended his arm toward a table with four chairs, the way a host in a fine restaurant might. He pulled out Abbey's chair for her. "Such a gentleman! Thank you!" Abbey said to Tom. She had forgotten for a moment, that this *gentleman* had violently killed people, including his own parents.

Jeff was just about to break through the awkwardness by starting the conversation, when Tom looked up at the ceiling. He swayed back and forth slightly, and smiled warmly. Then, a look came to his eyes – it was a look of innocent serenity. "Ticka, ticka, ticka. That's wonderful.

Of course!" Tom whispered, almost too softly to hear, as he looked at the ceiling.

Nick and Abbey wondered what he was doing, but neither of them asked. After all, he *did* live in the State Hospital for the Criminally Insane.

"Don't worry." Jeff said. "Tom does that sometimes. He finds it soothing."

Tom looked at Nick and Abbey with an intimate smile, as if they were his closest friends in the world. "That is such wonderful news for the both of you." He said.

For a moment, Nick, Abbey and Jeff assumed that he was referring to their desire to buy Knob Hill, but then he surprised them all.

"I have no doubt that you'll make wonderful parents!"

"Uhh...thank you, Tom, but we're not expecting." Abbey said. Her smile did not mask her confusion.

"Oh, but you *are* pregnant!" Tom said gently. "The mansion – the beautiful scrolled woodwork whispered it to me."

Nick and Abbey looked at Jeff. Neither one knew what to say, so they hoped that Jeff would bail them out of the awkward situation.

Jeff's brow was furrowed. He took a deep breath, and said, "Tom has an amazing intuitiveness, that he says comes from the mansion talking to him. It's weird, but I believe him. He knows things – things that he shouldn't know."

If it was anyone else, or anything other than the surreal situation that they were caught up in, Nick and Abbey would just write it off as the babblings of a guy who probably has schizophrenia. But, no. Nothing could surprise them now – or so they thought.

"You think that you need Knob Hill." Tom said to them. "And yes, you do. But in reality, it's Knob Hill that needs you. The mansion chose you – the three of you – only you can pull it from the darkness into the light."

"So, you're OK with the selling of Knob Hill?" Nick asked, hoping for a simple yes or no, because everything else was starting to creep him right out of his skin.

"Of course!" Tom said. "Like I said, the mansion chose you. It chose you long before you ever laid eyes on it."

CHAPTER 56

"Well, guys, here's where the rubber meets the road." Pete said as he and Nick worked the grill, and Abbey sat at the counter behind them. I had no idea that we would be closing on the place so soon. I guess paying cash can sure speed thing along."

"Yeah, I know. I was just thinking the same thing." Nick said. "We gotta help Dad get these short order cooks trained and all. It's less than a week till we bail on him."

Lou Davis overheard his sons from the back room where he was checking in a delivery. He stuck his head

297

through the doorway to the kitchen, and said, "I wish you two bone heads would stop sayin' that you're bailing on me! You're not! I've been wantin' this for the three of you, just as much as you have. You'll see – when you have kids." Lou said, giving them that look over the top of his reading glasses again.

"We love you too, Pop!" Nick said as he tapped his chest with his hand like a love-filled heartbeat.

"See, there ya go! If you goofs woulda done this sooner, maybe my hair wouldn't be so gray!" Lou said with a chuckle.

As soon as the old man walked away, Pete looked around, and then leaned across the counter as if he were getting ready to tell Nick and Abbey a juicy secret. "I'm almost afraid to ask, but did you take a pregnancy test yet?"

"Of course not." Abbey replied in a quiet voice.

"I...I don't think that we should scoff and brush off the things that Tom said, as being crazy." Pete said. "I mean, think about all the crazy-ass shit that has happened to us. All of it revolves around him and Knob Hill, so I'm thinking that Tom Willis might be the only one who really understands exactly what is happening!"

# OMINOUS WHISPERS

"So then, you're saying that I should run out and get a pregnancy test?" Indignation blended with fear and denial, swirled around in Abbey's mind, and caused her voice to rise, attracting the curious ears of some of the people in the diner.

"Shh." Nick said to Abbey, putting a finger to his lips. We'll wind up in the nut house if people hear what we're saying!"

Abbey nodded her head, and whispered, "OK. Sorry." Then she sat and stared at her husband with a look that said, *well?*

Nick sighed, and let the words that he thought, but did not want to say, come out. "Yeah! I do think that you should take a pregnancy test! There. I said it!"

"I don't think that we need to do that. I mean, my period isn't due for another three or four days, so why don't we just wait. If I get my period – which I will – then we won't have to worry about this nonsense!"

Abbey knew that it was not nonsense. She was trembling inside, like a dog going to the vet. She put her head in her hands, rubbed her face, and wondered why – *why me? Why Nick and Pete? Why is all of this déjà vu and past lives stuff happening to us?* She looked up and said, "OK. I'll pee on a stick."

TAMMY GACH

CHAPTER 57

Four days came and went, and no *visit from Aunt Flo*. Under any other circumstances, Abbey would be praying – willing the outcome to be the one she desired. But, not this time. This time, she honestly had no idea what she desired – she only had fear. Nick sat on the edge of the bathtub, while Abbey sat on the toilet, peeing on the pregnancy test stick.

"Maybe it's still too early for the test to be reliable." Nick said, wringing his hands, beads of sweat beginning to glisten on the bridge of his nose and his forehead.

Abbey hoped that she would not have to repeat the test. Once was enough. She felt like she was drowning in a sea of anxiety, and she really did not want a repeat. "This one says that it's accurate from the first day of a missed period." The sharp tone of her words told Nick that she did not want to hear anything that would add to her stress.

"I know, honey. I'm sorry." Nick said. He stretched his neck from side to side, hoping that each *crack, crack, crack* would relieve some of his tension.

Whether they knew it or not, Nick and Abbey were on the same page. They both wanted children, but the timing sucked. Starting a new business, especially in the *déjà vu house*, as Pete had started calling it, would be tough, even without a pregnancy. But, they would be thrilled, and they would find a way to make it work.

*A pregnancy now, especially while I'm on the pill, would be very unlikely – less than a one percent chance. And, it would mean that somehow Tom was right – that he knew I was pregnant – before it was ever even on my radar. Could it be possible? Could Tom have some kind of symbiotic relationship with the mansion? Could the deja-fucking-vu house really communicate with him? Why not?* Abbey thought. *Why not add a little more craziness to the growing heap of crazy that was already piling up?*

Holding their breath, Nick and Abbey watched the pink line form and become darker, beneath the word "pregnant" on the stick.

## TAMMY GACH

"You certainly have a big smile on your face today, Tom!" The nurse said as he got to the front of the line to get and take his meds.

"Yes Ma'am! I'm smiling because I know that there are parents out there – out there in the world right now – who love their children, and would never dream of hurting them."

The normally expressionless woman, known only as "Nurse" to the patients, smiled and said, "Yes, there are. What a lovely and positive thought, Thomas!"

OMINOUS WHISPERS

CHAPTER 58

"Honey! Come on now! You know I don't want you working so hard, and carrying a bunch of heavy stuff!" Nick scolded Abbey as she waddled, hugely pregnant, toward the restaurant kitchen with two boxes of newly delivered silver place settings and candle sticks.

"Yeah, yeah, blah, blah." She said. "They're not that heavy, and I'm not that delicate!"

The further along Abbey was in her pregnancy, the harder it became for Nick to know if she was joking, or actually irritated with him. "Be that as it may, you don't want to end up going into labor a month early, do you?" Nick said, carefully choosing his words. Abbey was not the type of woman to act weak or clueless in order to avoid hard work. And she sure as hell would not put on that kind of act in order to manipulate a man. Timid Abbey did not exist anymore. The car accident and painful rehab, had killed every last shred of self-doubt and weakness left in her.

"He's right, Abbey!" Pete chimed in with a laugh. "If you pop out my niece or nephew today, we won't get any more work out of you at all! And worse than that, I won't win with the baby squares that I picked!" He joked.

Nick laughed. "How many baby squares have you sold, Pete?''

"So far, $300 worth. That'll be $150 for the baby's college fund, and $150 for the winner!"

"How does that work, again?" Abbey asked.

"Well, it's like football squares, except it's not teams and scores. The baby squares are date of birth across the top, and hour of birth down the columns. People buy squares based on the date and time they think the baby will be born, and the closest one splits the pot." Pete said.

# OMINOUS WHISPERS

Abbey walked over to where the guys were working in the main dining room, which was once the mansion's formal living room. She sat down, and wiped her forehead. "OK, since you put it that way, Pete, I'll behave and stop lifting heavy things." She smiled and threw a work rag at her brother-in-law's head. Aside from the occasional crankiness that came from being uncomfortably huge in the last trimester of pregnancy, she was as happy as she had ever been. She was working with her two best friends in the world, her husband and his brother, to open the restaurant that they had always dreamed of, and she had a new baby on the way! *I am one lucky gal!* She thought.

"You know guys, we've been here working, cleaning, decorating for what? Seven – eight months now-and I haven't had a single déjà vu, or strange pain, or chill, or anything. How about you guys?" Sandy asked.

"No, I haven't either. I've been afraid to say anything about that, because I didn't want to jinx it!" Nick said.

"Me too! Maybe we've just been too busy to notice anything strange. After all, we have busted our asses to get this place up and running before the baby comes." Pete added.

"Yeah, and we're gonna do it too! We didn't give ourselves a hell-of-a-lot of time to get it up and running, but we'll make it! Unless, of course, the baby comes before opening day next weekend." Nick gave Abbey a teasingly stern look. She recognized it as the same – over the top of the reading glasses look that his father would give him and Pete. It made Abbey smile to wonder if her child would look at his or her children like that someday.

"Alright, alright – geez – I'll keep my legs crossed until after the grand opening!" Abbey joked. "Anyway…here's the idea I wanted to run by you guys. I've been thinking about what my dad has been saying about the mansion's creepy history, and how we could use it in marketing. You know how people are fascinated by the macabre, and by haunted places, and such? What if we added to the mystery and allure by naming the different dining and bar areas? Like the bedroom that Shatsworth was killed in – we could call it something like…*The Death by Seduction Suite*. You get the idea?"

"I think it's a brilliant idea!" Pete beamed. I can get Dad's buddy, Phil, down at the trophy shop, to do a rush job on some plaques to hang in the rooms, with the room name and a little history behind it. As long as we can get it together quickly, and don't go overboard naming every room, I think it's doable by the opening!"

## OMINOUS WHISPERS

"See, haven't I always told you, Pete? My beautiful wife is the smartest one of us all!" I love the idea, Abbey! Nick said, then he cocked his head. "I just hope that the Mansion likes the idea, and doesn't start *fighting back*."

CHAPTER 59

"These plaques came out beautifully!" Abbey said as she and Pete took them out of the protective bubble wrap.

"They sure did! We oughta send Phil a bottle of Scotch or something for finishing these on such short notice!" Nick said as he went to grab his cordless drill.

The *Whispering Specter Room* plaque went up first, in the music room, which was now the second largest dining area in the mansion. *On quiet evenings, it has been said, beautiful voices of musically inclined, singing specters can be heard coming from the intricately scrolled woodwork of this original music room.* Next, a large brass on mahogany plaque that simply read, *SPIRITS,* was hung over the door to the study which now contained an antique mahogany bar in addition to the original trappings of Simon Shatsworths manly pursuits – the exotic animal heads on the walls, the low tables with their legs made from elk forelegs, that sat in front of the leather couches, and the gun cases, filled with rare and antique rifles, pistols, and shotguns – except – of course – the one that Tom used on that awful, awful day in 1978.

Nick and Pete hung the plaques for the other four named rooms, under Abbey's direction. *Deadly Seduction Suite* in the small dining area that had once been the bedroom of Ansley Shatsworth, who was killed – presumably by his older brother, when the brother discovered that Ansley was having an affair with his wife. *Swan Dive Peak*, was now the name of another of the smaller rooms that would be used for afternoon tea. It was originally the bedroom, which had a perfect view of the roof peak, from which Ilse Shatsworth jumped to her death. A plaque that read, *Water Crypt Overlook*, told the story of the people who were killed, then put into cars and driven into the pond at the bottom of the hill. It was hung in the outdoor balcony area that overlooked the pond. Nick, Abbey and Pete still were not sure if they were going to keep that plaque or not. And finally, the Plaque that read, *You Only Live Twice Cigar Bar*, was hung in a room that was originally the servant's quarters. Nothing tragic – that they knew of – happened in that room. They just thought it would be a fun name.

# OMINOUS WHISPERS

## CHAPTER 60

*Tom...Tom.* The euphonic voice tickled his ear, just as he was drifting off to sleep. At first, Tom thought that he was asleep, and that he was dreaming – but no. The mansion was talking to him again.

"Yes, I'm here! I can hear you!" Tom sat up in bed. There was a radiant glimmer of hope and joy in his eyes, as he swirled his fingers through the air, almost able to feel the soft curves of her scrolled woodwork on his fingertips. His beloved mansion was talking to him again. After months of slumberous silence, Tom began to wonder if the mansion would forever be under the spell of Morpheus, and that he would never again hear its sweet sounds.

# TAMMY GACH

*Evil is here tonight Tom. It's wafting through the dining room, into the walls, polluting as it seeps down to my bones.*

"But they're dead!" Anger resonated through his voice. He knew that he needed to tone the volume down. If the night nurse heard him, it would earn him a shot in the ass of Haloperidol.

*Evil will never die, Tom. It takes many forms, and can darken anyone's soul. When an evil soul dies, there is always another, lying in wait, to replace it. But, don't despair, and try to sleep, Tom. Love and benevolence have already washed away so much of the slimy residue that infiltrated, and nearly destroyed me.*

Tom snuggled under his blanket, and the beautiful sounds of the mansion hummed a soothing melody to fill his ears, and calm his soul.

OMINOUS WHISPERS

CHAPTER 61

"For Christ's sake! I don't know why everyone raves about this place. It's a gimmick, that's all it is! It's only been open a week! You mark my words – This place will fold within a year – two max! And why do they keep it like a fucking meat locker in here!" City councilman, Ralph Penchant, growled across the table to his wife.

# TAMMY GACH

Lisa Penchant opened her mouth, and was about to say, *It's not cold in here,* but she thought better of it. It would open the door to a certain beating when they got home.

"Hey! Boy!" Ralph yelled to a young waiter, halfway across the dining room.

"Yes, Sir. How may I help you?" The sun tanned young man asked, as he backed up a step and discretely glanced down at his crotch. He thought that his fly might be open, because of the way that the obnoxious man at the table was staring at it.

"Well, you can start by turning that damned air conditioning down." Ralph said as he brushed his grease laden comb-over back into its place over the bald spot. "Can't you see my wife's about to freeze to death?"

"Certainly, Sir."

"Mr. Davis." The waiter softly said as he approached Pete.

"What's up, Jimmy?"

"Is it cold in here to you? One of the guests just complained that it's too cold in here."

"Which table, Jim? I'll go over there and check it out."

"Table thirty-two, Mr. Davis."

314

# OMINOUS WHISPERS

"Good evening, Sir…Ma'am. We've adjusted the air conditioning. It should warm up a bit for you in just a few minutes. May I get you a complimentary cocktail?" Pete asked with a smile.

"It's the least you can do!" Penchant grumbled. His meek wife glanced up at Pete, with a look in her eyes that clearly showed that she was mortified by her husband's behavior.

Pete came back to the table with the two vodka martinis with blue cheese olives that Penchant requested. As he was about to set them down, he was thinking, *double adulteration. First, ruin a perfectly good martini by using vodka instead of gin, then, add the taste of moldy cheese!* Pete knew that most people prefer vodka to gin in a martini, and that blue cheese olives were all the rage, but, for the life of him, he could not imagine why.

He served Mrs. Penchant first, but when he set Mr. Penchant's martini on the table in front of him, Pete felt air so cold that it pricked the skin on his hand.

"I think you're lying to me, Boy! I don't feel a damn bit warmer. If anything, it's colder in here than it was before! Now I suggest that you fix the fucking thing before you drive all of your customers out!"

TAMMY GACH

Pete looked up, thinking there must be a draft from above hitting that spot. When he saw no possible source of a cold draft, it hit him, causing his heart to skip a beat. *Oh shit!* He thought, quickly making his way to the kitchen to talk to Nick.

Mrs. Penchant, thin and typically cold, sat warm and comfortable in her high back wing chair at their table, watching her husband, sitting in an identical chair, scowling, shivering, and starting to turn a bit blue around the lips. *Oh dear God. Please, please let him be having a heart attack!"* She thought.

Lisa Penchant had grown to hate her husband. She probably would have poisoned the son-of-a-bitch by now if she thought that she could get away with it. She knew that he had been molesting boys for years – This was not the first time that she had walked in on him in the act. It was the same revolting pattern every time. She would walk in on him, he would give her smug smile, and when he was done, he would threaten the boy, and then he would threaten her. Once his dominance was established, he would throw her a bone – a trinket of costume jewelry, or a dinner out. By the next day, he would act as if nothing had ever happened. She learned early on not to bring it up. He would fly into a rage of denial, calling her a *crazy woman – plagued by menopausal hallucinations.*

316

# OMINOUS WHISPERS

There was no denying what she saw when she came home early from work today. There was Ralph, sitting on the edge of their bed, panting and wheezing like a bloated goat, with his hands gripping the hair of a twelve year-old neighbor boy, as he forced the boy's head back and forth, as the kid was gagging on her husband's penis.

She looked at him, barely able to hide her disgust as he popped a blue cheese olive into his filthy mouth. She knew that she should have stormed out and called the police. She could have. She had time to run, because, just like every other time, even though Ralph knew that his wife had caught him in the act, he did not leave the bedroom until he was finished with the boy. This time, once Ralph's perverse lust was satisfied, and the boy ran from the house, Ralph casually walked into the kitchen, where his wife was sitting at the table crying.

"I'll tell you the same thing that I told that little piss ant. If you go telling anyone, I'll kill you and chop you up into so many pieces that they'll never find you! And I'm gonna add one more thing for you," Ralph said smiling and stroking his wife's hair. "Don't you dare think about leaving me - I'll kill you for that too. Funny thing," he added. "You'd think that boy's father would keep a closer eye on him, seeing how he used to do the same thing for me when he was about that age."

# TAMMY GACH

Mrs. Penchant wiped her tears away, and managed a slight smile while she fought the urge to vomit. "OK. I won't tell, and I won't leave." Was all she could say, and her voice cracked when she said that.

"Now, what's the name of that dammed new restaurant that you've been bellyaching about? Get dressed and I'll take you there, you know, for having to see that, and all." He waved his hand to dismiss her.

Sitting at their table in the *Whispering Specter Room* of the Knob Hill Mansion Restaurant, Mrs. Penchant tried to drown her pain in her martini as she waited for her consolation dinner. Suddenly, she was pulled from the safe haven of her mind, by an unexpected shock. The table tipped, spilling her martini down the front of her dress, and Ralph's chair fell back, as he bolted up from it, holding his hands to his throat. Pete had just finished telling Nick about the freezing cold air that surrounded the man at table thirty two, when they heard the crash in the dining room. They ran to him and they realized that he was choking. A doctor, who happened to be dining there that night, ran over and started doing the Heimlich maneuver, but it was not working. Ralph Penchant's face was swollen and purple as he crumpled, unconscious to the floor. Pete called 911 from his cell phone, as the doctor continued to try to dislodge the blue cheese olive from Bob's throat.

# OMINOUS WHISPERS

"You!" The doctor said, pointing to Nick. "Get me a sharp knife – a filet knife, a heavy duty straw or tube, and some towels. Now!"

In the thirty seconds or less, that it took Nick to come back with the makeshift tracheotomy supplies, Ralph had gone into cardiac arrest, and the doctor was doing chest compressions. The paramedics arrived and took over the compressions as the doctor performed a crude tracheotomy.

Forty-five minutes later, a doctor escorted Mrs. Penchant into a private consultation room off the main waiting room of the hospital emergency department.

"We tried everything, Mrs. Penchant, but we just couldn't bring him back. I'm terribly sorry for your loss. Is there anyone we can call for you?" The doctor said softly, his hand on her shoulder.

"No. Thank you. I've already called my sister. She's on her way."

The doctor nodded, and then walked away. Mrs. Penchant smiled. *I'll be damned!* She thought. *A blue cheese olive! Who could have imagined! I guess bad things do happen to bad people.*

# TAMMY GACH

Nick and Pete gave free dinner vouchers to the patrons who remained, then they closed up early to have a cleaning service come and take care of the blood on the dining room carpet that remained from Ralph's futile tracheotomy. The brothers knew that it was the same freezing cold air that they felt in the basement, that day, years earlier, when they explored the mansion with Abbey. Neither had to say a thing.

Tom snapped to, from a deep sleep, and sat straight up in his hospital bed again.

*Now, now, Tom. Back to sleep you go. Everything is right as rain again.* The mansion whispered its soothing message in Tom's ear. *It's all better now. The evil is gone.*

Tom smiled and gave a sigh of relief, as he snuggled back down into his warm, safe bed, just like a child who has been reassured by a parent that there is not a monster under their bed.

OMINOUS WHISPERS

CHAPTER 62

"Bob! Bob! Vincent, the maître d', said with an air of urgency as he hurried into the kitchen from his usual post at the entrance to the restaurant. B.O.B was the nickname of affection that the staff had given to Nick and Pete – Boss and Other Boss. Typically the moniker was said with a laugh during a jovial moment, but this time Vincent sounded serious. "Mrs. Abbey – she's on the phone – she wants you home – it's time!"

"Oh boy!" Nick said, as he started a directionally confused pace about the kitchen. "Ah...ah...Pete!" He said.

## TAMMY GACH

"Yeah, I got it, Brother. You go home, take care of your wife, and we'll hold down the fort here – remember, just like we practiced!" Pete said, giving Nick a bear hug that lifted him off the ground.

Nick grabbed his car keys from the office. Instead of leaving through the side entrance, as usual, Nick stepped into the main dining room, and announced, "I'm gonna be a dad! Desert's on the house tonight!" His joy was met with cheers and applause from the guests and the employees.

"Man, I wish he'd have a baby every night that I work," Jimmy said to the rest of the wait staff at the end of the night. "I got three times more in tips than usual!" He gave a victorious downward punch in the air.

"Yeah, me too!" Amanda said, as the entire wait staff gave high-fives to each other.

Pete was excited, and anxious to get word from Nick about the baby, but not too distracted to notice the general feeling of euphoria that flowed through the mansion, seemingly affecting every person in the place on that particular evening. He felt happy and energetic – happier than he had in a while, and it made him realize - *This beautiful, wonderful, scary, confusing place, is a place of extremes. It lives and breathes the emotions of the people*

322

*within its walls, and then it feeds it back to them. She gives what she gets.*

His realization gave him a warm feeling of comfort, deep in his core, which he soaked in, until his phone vibrated in his shirt pocket. "Hello?"

"You're an uncle, Pete! You have a nephew! At 10:04 p.m. our beautiful, healthy nine pound, blonde haired baby boy was born!" Nick said.

Tears rolled down Pete's face, and the lump in his throat made it hard to express the joy that he was feeling.

"Abbey was great, man! She's good, and the baby's good! Dad's here, and Abbey's parents! I just can't believe it!" Nick beamed.

Pete could tell by the sound of his brother's voice and breathing that he was literally jumping up and down with happiness – just like he did when he married Abbey.

"I'm gonna head over there to the hospital as soon as I lock up. I can't wait to meet the newest little Davis dude! Give Abbey a kiss for me!" Pete said, smiling from ear to ear.

Pete was just about to leave the mansion and head to the hospital, when he remembered the baby squares. He pulled the well-worn piece of paper from his wallet, and scanned with his finger to the date and time. "Woo Hoo!" he jumped in the air and shouted. One of the squares he had picked was May 18$^{th}$ at 10:00 p.m., and the baby was born May 18$^{th}$ at 10:04 p.m.! "I won!"

OMINOUS WHISPERS

CHAPTER 63

*Sleep precious boy, sleep.* The song was soft and lovely and oh-so very soothing as it whispered in Tom's ear, lulling him deeper and deeper into sleep. *Feel the love fill your heart the way it was meant to. A nurturing, protective love – nature as she ensures that the cycle will continue. Join the majority, Tom. Join them, as you have now experienced as they have.*

Tom could feel his entire body – not just his fingertips - softly and slowly gliding along the scrolls of the woodwork of his beloved piano room. The scrolls held him in warm security as he drifted deeper and deeper into the sweetest surrender he had ever known.

OMINOUS WHISPERS

CHAPTER 64

No big surprise that Bob Penchant's prediction was wrong, and that Richard Duggan's was right. The Mansion at Knob Hill – Restaurant and Piano Bar was a huge success. The stories told by patrons, of hearing and seeing singing specters, and seeing a woman in a flowing black gossamer dress standing on the roof peak, were nothing more than figments of active imaginations, or exaggerations to spook their friends – but, fact or fiction, those were the stories that drew people in, and the food and atmosphere kept them coming back.

## CHAPTER 65

"*Ticka, ticka, ticka, ticka, ticka*" little three year old Eddie chattered as he ran his fingers, sticky from grape jelly, softly along the smooth, hand carved wood grillwork that separated the piano room from the living room.

Those words. Those made-up words stopped his parents in their tracks. They had heard them before, but at first, they could not recall where or when. Nick remembered a split second before it dawned on Abbey. It sent a surge of cold through both of them, like ice in their veins. Nick dropped his laptop computer that they had been using to create that day's menu, right where he stood. He scooped Eddie up in his arms.

"What did you say, Honey? Tell Mommy and Daddy." Eddie had not expected this sudden swoon of excitement from his parents. He was teetering on the verge of either crying or laughing, and the look on their faces would tell him which it would be. Abbey managed to smile at her son, aware that he was studying their faces.

Daddy's expression was not quite as reassuring as Mommy's, but Eddie held back the big alligator tears that were beginning to well up in his innocent blue eyes. After all, Daddy was the fun parent. The one who held him high in the air, flying him around the room like an airplane. Mommy, on the other hand, while not quite as fun as Dad, was his rock. She provided comfort and safety, like a calm harbor in a stormy sea. He trusted her. He was loved, and safe, and he knew it.

"What were you saying over there where you were playing, Sport? Were you talking to Mommy and Daddy?" Nick asked Eddie, hoping that it was just a bizarre coincidence.

"No, Daddy. The wood – the house wood. It talked to me! Daddy's a goose, Mommy." Eddie laughed with glee, the way he always did when he and Mommy would call Daddy a 'silly goose.'

"Daddy *is* a silly goose!" Abby playfully said, before asking the question that neither she, nor Nick really wanted answered. "What did the house wood say to you?"

"It told-ed me that *ticka, ticka* is ok to say, and you won't be mad." Eddie wiggled to be put down on the floor. Daddy was holding him too tight.

Nick and Abbey looked at each other. Silent for a moment. Both feeling like they had been sucker-punched in the gut. "Tom! That's the same damn odd-ball thing that he was saying when we went to see him at the psych prison!" Abbey half whispered, and half hissed in Nick's ear, as she tried not to let Eddie hear or see that she was becoming frantic.

"I know! And, he said that his mother got mad whenever he said it!" Nick whispered as he led his wife by the arm to the other side of the room. Out of Eddie's ear shot.

"You don't think it's happening again, do you?" Abbey asked her husband. *Nick always knows what to do*, she told herself, praying that he had a logical explanation. *He saved my life for God's sake! Not only that, but I would*

330

*only have one arm if it wasn't for him!* This, however, was beyond his control, and she knew it.

"I gotta get answers!" Nick said. He was not whispering now, but he was not shouting either. He paced in front of Abbey, as if he were a caged tiger that she was watching from behind bars.

Abbey knew that she had to be the stronger of the two of them at that moment. Despite everything that they had been through, and how terrified she had once been of the house, she knew; in the deep recesses of her mind, she knew that it was *the house* that dragged her back and forced her to rediscover the fierceness of her strength, and the intensity of her love.

"I'll give Jeff Bane a call – see if he or Tom might have some insight into this, of if we're just overreacting to a toddler's active imagination.

TAMMY GACH

CHAPTER 66

Abbey pulled the piece of paper with Jeff Bane's contact information that she had printed nearly four years earlier, from her file cabinet. She had hoped that she would never need it again, but something in the back of her mind told her that she would.

"Hello?" A man's voice answered. It sounded like him, but it had been a while.

"Jeff? Jeff Bane? It's Abbey Davis – at Knob Hill."

"Abbey! Lovely to hear your voice! I've heard that the restaurant is going gangbusters!"

# OMINOUS WHISPERS

"Thank you, Jeff! Yes, it is going quite well – but there is another reason for my call." Abbey chuckled nervously, and said, "I was just about to say 'this may be hard to believe', but then I remembered that you've seen some pretty incredible things too."

"Oh, indeed I have. You must be talking about Tom. I had a feeling when I heard your voice, that it was more than just a social call." He said.

"I was wondering if we could visit Tom, or maybe you could ask him something for us, because he was right about me being pregnant, and now our three year old son, Eddie, is running his fingers along the woodwork in the piano room, saying ticka, ticka, and telling us that the wood is talking to him, and it's freaking us out, and we want to know if Tom might know something about this."

There was momentary silence on Jeff's end, as he took a deep breath and rubbed his temple. "I would ask him, but I'm sad to say that my brother passed away in his sleep, a little over three years ago." Jeff said.

"Oh, Jeff. I'm so sorry for your loss." Abbey replied. She paused for a moment, and then finally, she asked, "What do you think, Jeff? I mean, what do you think Tom would say? You knew him better than anyone."

TAMMY GACH

"Thank you. And I'm glad you called, Abbey. Because, yes, I did know him better than anyone, and I can tell you that no matter what people think, my brother was not a monster. He was a kind, sweet soul who was abused and broken, and he simply snapped. So if you and Nick are worried that your little boy might have something evil in him from that house, or even from Tom, I don't think that you have anything to worry about. That house, or the spirit or soul, or whatever it is about that house, it loved Tom and tried to save him. The evil people who lived there – his parents, and the Shatsworths – they caused almost every bit of evil that ever occurred there. As much as I never want to see that place again, I have to believe that evil doesn't exist there anymore."

"Oh, thank you, Jeff. It puts my mind at ease to hear you say that. It's what I thought too, but hearing Tom's words, and seeing his mannerisms in Eddie – well, it just threw us for a loop. And I am sorry to hear about Tom's passing. How long has it been?

"Let's see, a little more than three years – yeah – May 18, 2014." Jeff said.

A shock ran through Abbey's body as if a giant icy hand gripped her chest. "May 18, 2014, you said? What time?" Abbey barely got her words out.

334

## OMINOUS WHISPERS

"It was late evening when they called me. Hold on, I have his death certificate here in my files."

Abbey held her breath. Through the phone, she could hear Jeff rifle through his papers. It seemed like an eternity.

"OK, here we go." Jeff said. "Time of death, 10:04 p.m."

Abbey dropped the phone.

Nick ran to her side. "Are you OK?" He asked.

Abbey simply nodded and picked up the phone. She could hear Jeff asking if she was still there. "Yes, I'm here." She said. Then she forced the words that she did not want to say. "Tom died at the exact time and date that our son was born."

Now, Nick knew why Abbey had dropped the phone, and the same icy grip that clenched Abbey, was now clenching him. He began to cry, because he knew what it meant. He recalled the moment that he heard that the three slain teenagers were killed on the same day and year that he, Abbey and Pete were born, and he recalled the terror that filled him when they realized that they were indeed the same three reincarnated.

Abbey wrapped up the phone call with Jeff. She sat on the beautiful jewel tone Persian rug, next to where Eddie was playing with his toy cars. Nick sat down next to them, and looked at his wife, waiting for her to say something – anything – because he did not know what to say.

Abbey looked at Nick for a long while, then nodded her head, and quietly said, "Yes, Nick. I do believe that Tom is getting a second chance through Eddie, just like Ted, Sandy and Billy got a second chance through us."

Nick stood up, and began to pace again. "Maybe this place is evil – evil right down and into the God-forsaken ground that it was built on." He said as tears streamed down his red face.

"No, Nick! You're wrong and you know it!" She insisted. "You're just scared, and I don't blame you. But I am choosing not to be scared, because you know that I'm right. You remember what I told you at my parent's house – the evening we decided to see if we could buy the property, and you asked if I was afraid?"

Nick didn't answer. He just shrugged his shoulders in sad defeat.

"I said that I thought we'd be the perfect people to give the place a second chance because we could fill it with love. And now I believe that Tom is getting a second chance as well – a chance at a life filled with love and happiness." Abbey said, as she stood and gave her husband a reassuring look and wiped the tears from his cheeks.

"What if you're wrong?"

"I'm not! And, I'm not changing my thought on that. Evil people seeped into the walls and crevasses of this house while they lived here. Good exists here now, and the good will wash all of that evil away. You'll see.

# TAMMY GACH

# OMINOUS WHISPERS

Made in the USA
Columbia, SC
22 May 2023

16556494R00207